To the Moon and Back

N.R. WALKER

Copyright

Cover Art: Soxational Cover Art
Editor: Boho Edits
Publisher: BlueHeart Press
To the Moon and Back © 2023 N.R. Walker

ALL RIGHTS RESERVED:

WARNING

Intended for an 18+ audience only. This book contains material that maybe offensive to some and is intended for a mature, adult audience. It contains graphic language, and adult situations.

TRADEMARKS:

Blurb

Gideon Ellery had the perfect life. Nice house, great job, and a long-time boyfriend. But weeks after adopting his nephew, his boyfriend splits, leaving Gideon a single father to a newborn. Disillusioned, sleep deprived, and unsure how to navigate fatherhood, he's asked to return to the office. He's overwhelmed and at his breaking point.

Toby Barlow is back in Sydney after three years of studying, travelling, and nannying in the UK. He needs work and a place to live, and the perfect solution drops in his lap. After all, caring for a sweet-cheeked baby in a beautiful home owned by a gorgeous single man isn't exactly terrible.

Gideon isn't too keen to share his life with a stranger, but his need for help is dire. Sunshiny Toby isn't prepared for a grumpy Gideon or his utterly adorable son, Benson. Or how easily he slots into their lives. And Gideon isn't prepared for how much he needs Toby.

Or how much he wants him.

Neither is prepared for the complications of falling in love.

N.R. WALKER

TO THE MOON AND BACK

Chapter One

"YOU NEED SOME HELP."

Gideon sighed, exhausted. Actually, he was so exhausted, he needed a new word for it. He looked at Lauren and Jill, his dearest friends, and nodded. "I know."

Benson stirred, his waking grizzles clear through the baby monitor. "I'll get him," Jill said gently, and disappeared down the hall.

Lauren patted Gideon's knee. "It'll be okay," she reassured. "It's the right thing to do."

Gideon knew it was, even if it stung. He'd thought he could do it. Being left on his own with a six-week-old baby had been awful. Having his life upended, having his long-term partner simply walk out on them, had been *awful*. And after six weeks of trying to do it all—full-time work, full-time dad—it had just been too much. Lauren and Jill had helped immensely, but they couldn't do it forever. Gideon could barely keep his eyes open, and it was only a matter of time before something went wrong.

He needed to work to keep his house. Having a house—this house—to raise Benson in was important to Gideon,

1

and he'd worked remotely as much as his job would allow. His bosses had been gracious and generous, but he was drowning. The bottom line was, Benson needed better care. Gideon had relied on Jill and Lauren's help enough already. He needed a full-time solution.

"And this guy is good?"

Lauren nodded. "He has a degree in early child development. He's worked as a nanny in England for three years and is now back in Sydney. You know my boss and her level of standards."

Gideon nodded. Lauren's boss was a high-flying lawyer who accepted nothing but the best.

"She recommended him," Lauren added. "And he's available through the agency now. I know you didn't want just any old stranger. Senna said he's great. It's perfect timing."

Jill came out holding a fussing Benson. "Changed his nappy and he's good to go," Jill said, handing Benson to Gideon. "Think he wants his dadda."

Gideon took his son, holding him close and inhaling in the baby powder smell. He softly kissed his head, immediately rocking back and forth. "Dadda's got you."

Benson settled though Gideon kept rocking. He loved his son more than life itself. He'd never imagined loving any other person as much as he loved Benson. He was all he had now. It was just the two of them.

Getting help was the right thing to do. Not just for himself but for Benson too.

A nanny . . .

Gideon sighed again, resigned. Too exhausted to argue. "What time will he be here?"

Toby Barlow drove through the leafy suburban Putney streets, grateful for Siri's directions. He wasn't too familiar with this part of Sydney, given it'd been years since he'd been in Sydney, and the price range of the houses and cars he drove past were well and truly out of his league.

There were grassy parks with dappled shade from huge trees, people strolling with kids and dogs out enjoying the spring sunshine.

Could he live and work here?

Hell yes.

Well, if the guy he was meeting turned out to be an arse, he might decline. God knows the last family he'd worked for in London hadn't been a treat . . . Well, the kids were great, but the parents had been horrible. Horrible parents, horrible human beings.

Surely this guy couldn't be that bad.

All Toby knew of Mr Gideon Ellery was that he was thirty-four years old, a very well-established corporate finance manager, and a recently single new father to a twelve-week-old son.

Babies. Toby loved babies.

Toby pulled up at the address he was given. The house itself was a Victorian style bungalow with a cute front yard with grass and its very own tree, complete with an expensive black Audi SUV parked in the driveway.

He was used to working for, and living with, wealthy people. After all, who else could afford a full-time live-in nanny? He hoped his brother's little Corolla wouldn't make him look unworthy.

With a deep breath and a quick look in the rear-vision mirror to fix his hair and check that he had nothing stuck in his teeth, he got out and knocked on the front door. A woman with short blonde hair and a welcoming smile

3

answered. "Hi, my name is Toby Barlow," he said confidently. "I'm here to meet with a Gideon Ellery?"

"Yes, yes, please come in," she said, opening the screen door for him. "My name's Lauren. My boss is Senna Mardell. I believe you know her sister . . ."

Ah, the one who lined this up.

"Yes, yes, thank you," I said. "I looked after Senna's sister's children in London. She told me if I ever needed a reference . . ."

Lauren's smile widened even further. "Come on through. I'll introduce you."

The house was even more beautiful inside. Polished wooden floors, white walls, high ceilings, original filigree ornate woodwork infills. Toby dreaded to think what this house cost. They walked through to a lounge room where he was met by another woman—dark hair, nervous smile.

And a man sitting on the couch holding a baby boy.

"This is my wife, Jill," Lauren said. "Jill, this is Toby Barlow."

Toby shook her hand. The fact they were queer made Toby relax immediately. *It's always nice to be around your people.* He smiled wide. "Nice to meet you."

"Likewise."

"And this is Gideon," Lauren added. "And little Benson."

Gideon was . . . well, not what Toby had been expecting. He had short brown hair and a moustache to rival Tom Selleck.

A moustache? Oh yes.

Toby liked it. A lot.

But then he realised something else about Gideon.

The man was drained. He looked absolutely beat—dark circles under his eyes, puffiness, even a little pallid. He still managed to be good looking, Toby thought. Even with the moustache.

Especially with the moustache.

"Nice to meet you," Toby said. Gideon didn't offer his hand to shake. He was sitting down with a fussing baby after all, so Toby didn't mind.

"I'll make him a bottle," Jill said, disappearing into the kitchen.

"Let's sit down and have a chat," Lauren suggested, gesturing for Toby to take the single-seater. She sat beside Gideon and gave him a reassuring smile.

"Thank you for coming," Gideon said. His voice was a bit husky around the edges.

They made small talk about traffic until Jill reappeared with a bottle, and Toby took this as his opportunity. He offered Gideon his CV. "How about we swap? You can read over my credentials and let me take this little chicken nugget for you," he said, taking Benson. Jill handed him the bottle. Toby sat down and began to feed Benson.

Benson's big blue eyes stared up at him, long dark lashes, rosy cheeks, and a cute little button nose.

Benson was possibly the cutest baby he'd ever seen.

Toby looked up, smiling at his audience. Jill and Lauren were smiling fondly back at him, but Gideon was not. He sat there, holding the CV, staring at Toby.

"Chicken nugget?"

Toby's grin widened as he looked back down at the feeding baby. Benson, still looking up at him, giggled around the bottle teat. Toby laughed and nodded. "Chicken nugget."

Chapter Two

GIDEON COULDN'T DENY TOBY'S CV WAS GOOD. ALL his certificates were up to date, his police-check was fine. He had great experience, a degree in child development, he was bright and friendly and ultimately someone Gideon would have no problem in allowing to live in his house.

First impression was good. He was sharply dressed, professional-looking, with navy trousers and a white button-down shirt. He had dark hair—short but styled—dark brown eyes, and perfect teeth.

The way he took Benson so effortlessly, fed him, burped him, and made him smile and giggle. And not just that . . . but the way Toby smiled at Benson too. He was obviously great with kids. There was no doubt about it.

But *chicken nugget?*

He'd called Benson a chicken nugget.

"So you had two years with your first employer in London," Gideon said. It wasn't really a question.

"I did," he replied. "It was a two-year contract with three kids, ages newborn, two, and four. I adored them."

"That was Senna's niece and nephews," Lauren added, giving Gideon a pointed look.

"Yes," Toby said with a smile. "Lovely family. Nellie turned two just before I left. I loved them."

"And your next employment was just one year," Gideon said, looking at the dates on the CV.

"Yes. The contract was for twelve months, but full disclaimer—I cut it short at ten months."

"Why was that?"

Toby met Gideon's gaze and he held it. "The kids were great. Aged four and two. Just adorable. The parents . . . Well, let's just say we had a difference of opinion on a subject I wasn't prepared to ignore."

Gideon cocked his head. "Oh?"

"Yes," Toby stated coolly. "They were bigots. Racist and homophobic, so a double whammy, really." He made a face and shook his head. "I'm fine with differing opinions. I have no problem with that. But a difference of opinion is disagreeing on the horror that is coriander, not whether other people should be treated like human beings. That's a deal breaker for me. As it turned out, they had some pretty radical beliefs, and I'm more of a treat-everyone-like-a-human-being kind of person, so needless to say I couldn't bring myself to work for them any longer. I was due to come home in a few months anyway." He sat a little taller, still bouncing Benson on his lap, but he focused his gaze on Gideon. "There are very few things that I would terminate employment for. This is your home, your son, and I'll always be respectful of that, and I'd be employed to do a job. But I won't tolerate bigotry. Is that going to be a problem? Because if you'd prefer everyone in the world to be white and straight, then I won't waste any more of your time.

Well . . ." He waved a hand in the general direction of his face. "I'm white, obviously."

But not straight?

"I don't mind if you prefer coriander," Toby continued. Gideon wondered if he talked like this all the time or if he was a nervous rambler. "I can cook with it if you insist. I'd just prefer food that doesn't taste like soap. It's not a deal breaker, per se. But speaking of deal breakers, and though I don't have to disclose this, I'd prefer you to know up front that I am very much a six on the Kinsey scale. Which means gay, if you're not up to code. I'd just rather not have a repeat of my last experience."

Lauren pressed her lips together so she didn't smile too wide, but Jill just laughed and nudged Gideon. "I'm up to code," Gideon said flatly. "And, uh, no, that's not a problem. My partner—" He stopped himself. "My ex-boyfriend is a man, obviously. So yeah, it's not a problem for me." Gideon had wondered if any nanny might take issue with his sexuality. He hadn't even considered his nanny could also be gay. It certainly made things less awkward. Unless . . . "And I assume it's not a problem for you."

Toby waved his hand while gently bouncing Benson on his lap. "Oh, heavens, no."

There were contract rules about any nanny, male or female, bringing anyone back to the house, so it wasn't something that needed to be negotiated. If Toby didn't agree with that, he didn't get the job. Gideon was pleased about having a contract and agency, but he thought it best to bring up any queries.

"Do you have any questions about the contract?"

Toby shook his head. "No. It was all very straightforward; the agency looks after us both in that regard. But can I ask about the arrangements with the ex-partner?"

Gideon was immediately defensive. "Why?"

"Is it a shared custody arrangement? Weekends? Are there any court-issued arrangements I should be aware of? There wasn't anything in the contract."

Oh.

Lauren's smile was now gone. Jill shook her head but let Gideon speak. "There are no arrangements," he said. "Drew left us both—me and Benson—six weeks ago. He hasn't even asked to see him, never even asked about him. Not once."

"Asked for his vinyl collection, though," Jill said flatly.

Toby grimaced. "I'm sorry to hear that."

Even talking about it made Gideon itch to protect Benson. He stood up and crossed the living room and took Benson, holding him tight and giving his soft cheek a kiss. "It's just us now, isn't it, my little guy?"

Toby smiled up at them. "Well, he's just about perfect."

Gideon couldn't help himself. "Perfect as a chicken nugget?"

Toby surprised him by laughing as he stood up. "Exactly."

Then Lauren was standing as well. "How about you show Toby his bedroom," she said. Then quickly added, "If you both decide it's what you want."

Gideon had almost forgotten that part. "Yes, of course. This way," he said. "There are three bedrooms. Mine, Benson's, and the guest room." He opened a door on the hall to show a decent-sized room with a double bed and a built-in wardrobe. The walls were white, the bed cover was navy, and there were three white frames on the wall with different navy-coloured prints.

"It's lovely," Toby said quietly. He was impressed. Gideon noted that Toby didn't seem to be able to hide his

9

reactions very well. From his reaction to Benson, to the room just now, and from what he said about his last employer, Gideon liked that Toby said it as he saw it. "My last room in London was the size of a shoebox. Not an adult-sized shoebox either. You know those small boxes toddler shoes come in? Like that."

Gideon couldn't help but smile, but he went across the hall. "This is Benson's room."

Toby walked in, turned back, and gave Gideon and Benson a bright smile. "Oh my god. This is the cutest nursery ever!"

Gideon was smiling again, something he hadn't done a lot in these last weeks. "Thanks. It took a long time to get it right."

That wasn't exactly true. It had taken a long while for Gideon and Drew to agree on a theme. Drew wasn't happy with anything Gideon had suggested: themes, colours, designs.

As it turned out, Drew wasn't happy with a lot of things.

Gideon could see that now.

In the end Drew had said he didn't care about the 'stupid theme' and for Gideon just to do whatever he wanted. So he had.

And apparently Drew had too. Not the decorating; goodness, he'd done none of that. What Drew had wanted to do was leave. To find someone else and leave.

Gideon was still so angry about it. He was bitter and spitting mad. If he was following the stages of grief, then he was right on track. And he *was* grieving. He'd lost his boyfriend of six years, the family he'd wanted, the family they were. The life they were supposed to have.

He hated Drew. But he also still loved him, and it was a constant seesaw of heartache. Now every time he wanted to drown in the anger of it all, he shifted that energy into something positive for Benson.

Instead of yelling and screaming, he'd sing a song to Benson, give extra-long cuddles, or read books to him. Anything to distract himself, to benefit Benson, but also to make himself a better dad. To make up for the fact that he had to be twice as good now.

While he'd tried to do it all, Gideon didn't blame himself for not being a super-dad, and he certainly didn't blame Benson. Babies were innocent and, after all, a lot of work. He blamed Drew, one hundred percent.

"To the moon and back," Toby said, reading the decal above Benson's crib.

Gideon gave Benson another kiss on the cheek. "I tell him that every time I put him to bed," Gideon said. "And turn on this light," he said, pressing the switch on the small box on the chest of drawers.

The room went dark, with purple and blues swirling on the ceiling and walls, turning the whole room into a galaxy. "I play this every night when I put him to bed. I tell him stories and we look at the stars."

Toby's smile was warm and kind, and he gave Benson a gentle tweak on the arm. "Daddy's little astronaut."

Gideon snorted out a laugh. "Well, I guess that's better than chicken nugget."

Toby grinned. "He can be both. A cheeky chicky nuggy astronaut."

Gideon stared at him.

Oh sweet heavens, it was getting worse.

TOBY HAD ALMOST DIED OF CUTENESS OVERLOAD WHEN he walked into Benson's room. The walls were a duck-egg blue and there were space decals all over. Planets, stars, rocket ships; a bit like *The Little Prince*, but not really. Just the outlines, very trendy and gorgeous. Toby could guess that the whole room had been ridiculously pricey.

There was a spinning mobile of planets above the expensive crib, framed pictures that matched the decals, only in full colour, and big scroll writing *To the moon and back* surrounded by stars on the wall. There was even a small sofa that Toby imagined was used for night-time feeds, and the galaxy light was amazing.

It looked like something straight out of a design magazine.

Toby had been surprised when Gideon offered him the job, given Toby had word-vomited through most of his interview and Gideon clearly wasn't overly fond of Toby's habit of giving kids a nickname. But offered the job, he had.

Which was why, two days later, he moved in.

Granted, it was one suitcase and a carry-on, plus a bag with his laptop and a few personal effects. The beauty of living in other people's houses for the last few years was that Toby hadn't any need for furnishings or household items.

Or maybe it was a downside.

Everyone else he knew was renting their own place, had their own things.

Toby never felt it more than when he was either moving in or moving out of a job, though he was certain it would fade once he settled into his new routine. He'd unpacked and got everything settled all before 10:00 am and thought it would be best to get the awkward first day out of the way.

He headed out to the living area and found Gideon

almost pacing in the kitchen. He stopped when he saw Toby. "Oh, you get everything moved in okay?" he asked.

"Sure did."

"Benson's back down for a nap," he said. "Of a night, he'll sleep for five hours, wake around 2:00 am for a bottle, then goes back down for another four hours. Has his morning bottle, stays up for a bit, and goes back down just for a short nap. Sometimes around forty-five minutes." He produced some papers in a plastic sleeve. "Anyway, I've written down his schedule for you . . . Well, it's his schedule this week. Could be different next week. Actually, pretty sure it will be different next week. Maybe even tomorrow."

Toby took the schedule. He was certain he would have figured it all out, but he did appreciate the effort. "Excellent. Thank you."

"And there's general house stuff in there too," Gideon added. "Not rules or anything. Just the alarm code, and what day is bin day, and the Wi-Fi and Netflix password, that kind of thing."

"Oh, that's perfect, thank you."

"I tried to think of everything."

Gideon was so nervous, Toby wanted to squeeze him. "Can I make you a coffee or a cup of tea?" Toby offered. "It'll help me find my way around the kitchen, and then we can sit down and do some meal planning and a grocery list."

Not waiting for an answer, Toby filled the kettle, and he only had to open two cupboards before he found the coffee mugs. "Coffee or tea? I'm more partial to tea these days. Used to be a big coffee drinker, but living in England, I just found myself having pots of tea instead."

"Uh . . ." Gideon hesitated, then seeing Toby was just going right ahead and helping himself anyway, he answered. "Tea is fine, thank you."

It was why Toby did it. If he was going to be living here, then he *lived* here. Respectfully, of course. Making cups of tea and being comfortable around the home were important for Toby. And more often than not, it helped the family adjust as well.

They sat at the dining table with their cups of tea, and Toby pulled out his phone. "Shall we do some meal plans and make a shopping list?"

"Oh, uh, you don't have to do that," Gideon said. "I can organise that."

Toby resisted sighing. He needed to be patient with Gideon. It was his first time with a nanny, after all. And Toby didn't think it was because Gideon was a control freak. No, Toby was sure Gideon felt guilty for not doing every single thing.

"It's fine," Toby said brightly. "It's what I do. Cooking, cleaning, laundry. Whatever needs doing. Granted, Benson is my priority, so if he's having a miserable day, dinner could be tinned soup and toasted sandwiches."

Gideon almost smiled, but boy, did he ever look tired.

"I can make a vegetable pasta or a poached chicken dish. I make a pretty good curry," Toby said. "Do you have any allergies?"

Gideon shook his head. "No. None."

"Any dislikes or foods to avoid? Foods you love?"

He sipped his tea. "Coriander."

That made Toby smile. "Are you for or against?" He never did say the other day.

"Unequivocally, undisputedly against."

"Oh thank god," Toby breathed. "It's the worst. Actually, between that and kale, I don't know which one takes the trophy as the worst. They need a dual podium."

"I like kale."

Toby faked a gasp. "Nooo."

"Is that worse than a human rights violation?"

Toby squinted at him. "Not even close, but perhaps we could start a petition."

Gideon almost smiled. "Perhaps we could."

Toby liked that he could elicit an almost-smile from Gideon. He was clearly guarded, tired, and freshly heart-broken. His partner had deserted him—no, *them*—when Benson was just six weeks old.

Toby decided right then and there, sitting at the dining table with their cups of tea, that he would do everything he possibly could to make Gideon's life better.

"You're not working at all today?" he asked.

Gideon grimaced. "No, I . . . I thought I'd be here for the first day."

Toby nodded. "It's perfectly natural to be nervous and anxious about leaving Benson with a stranger. I get that. In fact, I'd be worried if you weren't."

Gideon inhaled and let it out slowly, turning the mug of tea in his hand, and he conceded a small nod.

Toby reached over and gave his forearm a squeeze. "You're a good dad."

Gideon's eyes flashed to Toby's, a deep and soulful grey. "Thank you."

Toby gave him the brightest smile he had, then tapped his phone screen. "So, let's make a shopping list. Then when Benson wakes up, we can take a walk down to the park and get to know each other a bit better. Then when we get home, we can all have some lunch, and when you and Benson have a nap, I'll go to the supermarket and get every-thing we need to make us dinner."

Gideon looked at him as if he'd sprouted a second head, but it just made Toby smile even more. "How does grilled chicken and salad for dinner sound?"

Chapter Three

GIDEON WASN'T SURE WHAT TO MAKE OF TOBY. HE WAS an organiser, that much was clear. He liked lists: to-do lists, shopping, meal planning, schedules. But it was more than that. He breezed through it all cheerfully. When Benson woke, Toby changed him, packed the nappy bag, loaded up the pram, and ushered Gideon out the door, all while smiling and singing to himself.

Effortlessly.

Gideon dreaded having to leave the house with Benson some days. Having to pack up his entire life just to go to the supermarket, only for Benson to decide he needed a bottle twenty minutes later . . . It was just all so hard and honestly, easier to just stay in.

Toby made it look so easy. He was humming away, smiling as he did six things at once, all while Gideon could barely muster the energy to put his shoes on.

Toby waited on the front porch with the pram, smiling brightly, as Gideon grabbed his keys and locked the door behind them, then they walked down to the park.

Gideon tried to remember the last time he'd walked to

the park. It was just down the street, one block away, yet Gideon never had the energy. He'd wanted to, before Benson arrived and they were making grand plans—correction—before Benson arrived and *he* was making grand plans. Gideon was sure they'd do all the family things: walks to the park, trips to the zoo, holidays . . .

The truth was, he couldn't even make it to the freaking supermarket.

Well, before Toby.

"This is such a gorgeous suburb," Toby said, pushing the pram. Gideon had to wonder if the guy ever stopped smiling. "I forgot how blue the sky was here. Three years in England and I almost thought the sky was supposed to be grey."

Toby never really gave Gideon a chance to speak. Whether he was trying to avoid awkward silences or if he always talked non-stop, Gideon wasn't sure. But he just kept on talking. "And the trees! Oh my god. They're just gorgeous. Are these all Moreton Bay Figs? They're huge, and they shade everything."

Gideon didn't even mind that Toby kept talking on and on as they got to the park. He didn't have the brain power for an in-depth conversation, so it was a relief to simply partake without the effort of more than one- or two-word answers.

Toby didn't seem to mind either. Hell, he didn't even seem to notice. He spread a blanket down on the shaded grass and took Benson out of the pram and gently laid him down in the middle of the blanket and gave him a brightly coloured caterpillar toy to play with.

Benson was so happy, kicking his little legs and babbling away, and Gideon instantly regretted not doing this sooner.

Toby sat with his legs outstretched and patted the

blanket next to Benson. He looked up at Gideon as if he were sunshine personified, and Gideon really wanted to dislike him.

He wanted to despise Toby, his demeanour, his positive outlook, his permanent smile, and bright eyes. The pessimist in Gideon wanted to roll his eyes and grumble at Toby's blinding optimism. He wanted to hate him for making it all look so easy.

But he couldn't.

There was warmth in that sunshine. There was light in that positive outlook. He hardly knew Toby at all, but there was something in that smile that made Gideon pause.

So Gideon sat himself down. Outside, in the fresh air. He'd almost forgotten that it existed. "Thank you for suggesting we do this," he said.

Toby smiled with a pleasant sigh as he looked out over the park, and Gideon studied his side profile, hating to admit Toby was kinda cute. "You're very welcome," Toby said, glancing his way with a peaceful smile. "And I'm glad you like it because I think we should do this all the time."

"WHAT DO YOU MEAN HE'S *MAGNUM PI* LEVEL OF hot?"

Toby pressed his phone to his other ear as he steered the shopping trolley. Of course he had to choose one with a wonky wheel. "What I mean," he whisper-hissed at his brother, "is that he's as hot as Magnum PI. This wasn't a difficult analogy, Josh."

"The new one or the old one?"

"There's a new one?"

"So the old one."

Toby stopped walking. He hadn't even made it through the fruit and vegetable section yet. "He's not old."

"The original Magnum PI is old, Tobes. Jesus, do you have a thing for the elderly?"

"I do not have a thing for the elderly," Toby snapped. Then he had to smile at a horrified little old lady who was just trying to pick a good bunch of celery. He moved along to the fruit section. "Tom Selleck was not old when he played Magnum PI. He was sexy as hell."

"I'm googling as we speak," Josh said. Toby could hear the tapping of keys. "Oh my. Those shorts are very short. Now, I'm not gay, but . . . does your new boss wear shorts like these?"

"Not the shorts," Toby replied. "How can you not notice the moustache? And no, he doesn't wear shorts like that. Not that I would mind terribly if he did. Just sayin'."

Josh laughed. "What about the floral shirts and hairy chest? Does your new boss have those too?"

"Not that I've seen." Then Toby reconsidered this as he picked up a bag of oranges. "Not that I'm looking."

Josh laughed. "Sounds like you're looking to me."

Adding some peaches and apples, Toby finished in the fruit section and moved onto the bread aisle. "I'm not looking. I cannot be looking. He's my boss, and today is technically my first day. I just needed to tell someone."

"You never mentioned any of this after your interview. You said he was genuinely nice and exhausted. There was no mention of a 1980s sex god."

Toby snorted. "I was trying to pretend I didn't notice. And speaking of exhausted, I should hurry and get back. I left them napping. I can't be dawdling, and you should be working too."

"You called me, remember? And I am working. You

called me *at* work. And how do you pay for those groceries? Does he give you his credit card?"

"No, he set up a separate charge card. Any and all expenses go on that," Toby said as he zipped into the next aisle. "God, why do supermarkets have to move where they put shit? I've been gone three years, and nothing is the same."

Josh laughed. "You have fun with that. We'll catch up when you get a day off. Do dinner or something."

"Sounds good."

"It's good to have you back in the country, little bro."

Toby hated when Josh called him that, but it was nice to be back. He'd missed his family terribly. He found himself smiling despite his annoyance. "It's good to be back. Where the fuck is the sweet soy sauce?"

He heard Josh laugh before the line went dead. Great. He looked up and straight into the face of a staff member. He was pushing a cage full of boxes and Toby thought he might have a dig at him for swearing, but nope. He just gave him a nod. "Aisle five."

Aisle five?

Oh, the sauce.

"Thank you!"

Toby got back to the house to find Benson still asleep and a barely awake Gideon. Whether he'd actually slept on the couch, Toby didn't know, but even if he caught ten minutes, it was better than nothing.

The man had serious dark circles under his eyes.

Toby put the two canvas bags on the kitchen bench and Gideon immediately went to help put things away. "Why don't you go take it easy," Toby suggested. "I can do this."

"Benson will be awake soon," he said.

"And I'll tend to him." Toby gave him a reassuring

smile. It was always hard for the parents to take that first step back. "Do you want me to make you a cup of tea while you tell me all about Benson's night-time routine? Bath, dinner, story time."

Gideon didn't seem to know what to do or say when Toby all but plonked him into a chair at the table with a fresh cup of tea. Toby put all the groceries away as Gideon explained his and Benson's nightly routine, and it wasn't long before Benson woke up.

"I'll get him," Toby said and was out of the kitchen before Gideon could stand up.

Benson went from grizzles to smiles as soon as he saw Toby. "This little cheeky chicken nugget knew he was getting busted out of jail as soon as he saw me," Toby said, handing him gently off to Gideon. "You go to your daddy, and I'll make you a bottle."

"Uh, I'm his dadda," Gideon said quietly.

Dadda. Okay, got it.

Everything about Gideon changed as soon as he held Benson. His whole face just radiated love. He held him as if he were the most precious thing in all the galaxy and looked at him with complete awe and wonder.

It was so very clear that Benson was Gideon's entire world, and it really warmed Toby's heart to see. Sure, it was only Day One, but Toby had a *really* good feeling about this job.

Chapter Four

GIDEON COULDN'T BELIEVE HOW EASY IT WAS. How good it was to have Toby. He'd been worried about the adjustment and had dreaded something awkward or terrible happening, but the first week was seamless.

The first night, Toby had cooked spaghetti Bolognese. Nothing extravagant, but delicious nonetheless, and although Toby had first suggested chicken and salad, he'd decided on pasta instead. And with a belly full of carbs and the first proper meal in far too long, Gideon had crashed and slept hard. Gideon was certain that was why Toby had opted for pasta.

Gideon didn't even remember falling asleep. He didn't remember getting into bed. He'd turned the light off and was out. Toby had said he'd take the first few nights to let Gideon get some much-needed sleep, and Gideon had agreed, assuming he'd hear Benson and get up regardless.

He hadn't heard a peep.

He'd woken up at 6:00 am with a start, panicked that something bad had happened, and instead, found a smiling Toby feeding Benson his bottle.

How could anyone be sleep rumpled and tired and still smile like that?

"I'm so sorry. I didn't hear him at all. Did he wake at two?" Gideon had scrubbed his hand over his face, trying to clear the fog. "My god. I've never not heard him before."

"It's fine." Toby had simply smiled like it was no big deal. He fed Benson, changed him, made himself some breakfast, and was having floor time with Benson when Gideon had left for work.

Gideon found it so hard to leave for work on that first day.

He'd phoned them at ten, then at one, and again at four. Of course, everything was fine. He could hear Benson babbling happily in the background, and Toby had put the phone closer so he could hear even better.

The second day wasn't any easier.

On the third day, Toby hadn't answered his one o'clock phone call. The phone rang out and Gideon's anxiety just about went into the stratosphere. He was half packed up and out the door when his phone rang with an incoming FaceTime.

Benson's happy face appeared on the screen, smiling and chewing on his favourite toy caterpillar. Gideon could see he was lying on the blanket Toby often spread out on the floor. "Say hello to Dadda," Toby said off-screen.

Of course, Benson never said a word, but Gideon had almost cried, sagging with relief.

"There's my little man," he managed to say.

Then Toby's face appeared on screen. "We thought a video call today was in order. Hope we didn't interrupt. I figured because you called, you were free. We just needed a nappy change first."

"I don't mind at all." Gideon's heart was . . . happy. He

hadn't been happy in far too long. Yes, he was happy with Benson, of course. But he hadn't felt joy. Joy was a better word. "Actually, I really appreciate it."

"Then we shall do it every day at one o'clock," Toby announced.

So they did.

It was the highlight of Gideon's day. Well, apart from getting home and seeing Benson smile when he saw him, or first cuddles after a long day. Or cuddles before bed, or story time, when Gideon would read soft and calming words to Benson as his little eyelids got heavier and heavier. Those were highlights too.

On Friday, just before his one o'clock lunch break, there was a soft knock on his office door. Lauren poked her head in. "Hello, stranger," she said. "Was literally walking past your building and thought I'd shout you some lunch."

"Sure," he replied. "Can you just give me ten? I'm about to get a very important call."

She took a step back toward the door. "Oh, I can come back—"

"No, come in." He waved her over just as the FaceTime call came in. Gideon answered and Benson's chubby, smiley face appeared. "Look who just woke up," Toby's voice said. "Say hello to Dadda."

Benson gurgled and babbled, his fist in his mouth.

Gideon could have just burst. "How's my beautiful boy?"

Toby replied even though Benson's face never left the screen. "You tell your dadda you're the best little chicky nuggy that ever nuggied."

Gideon smiled, not even mad. Lauren squeezed his arm, her smile warm. When the call ended, she patted his shoulder. "Let me buy you lunch."

He knew there would be a lot of questions, and thankfully she withheld them until they were sitting in the café and he'd had half his sandwich.

"So things are going well with Toby?" she began. It wasn't really a question.

He took a sip of his coffee and sighed. "He has been a godsend. I honestly cannot thank you and Jill enough for finding him."

Lauren smiled fondly at him. "You look like you've slept."

He almost laughed. "Toby said he'd do night shift this week. It's not in his contract to do that, but he offered, and honestly, I think he thought I needed it."

"You *did* need it. You were about to drop."

"A few proper nights' sleep and I feel like I could take on the world." He sipped his coffee again. "Well, I'm not dragging through each day in a daze. So there's that. And he's feeding me. Actual cooked dinners every night. I feel human again. And my time with Benson is . . . I don't know. I can appreciate it now. And that sounds weird, but up until Toby, everything was an effort. Now, I can enjoy time with him without worrying about the little stuff, and"—he shrugged—"not being dead on my feet helps."

Lauren studied him for a long second. "You look good, Gideon. I know you were worried, but I'm so glad it's working out." Then, with a certain tone, she added, "And I noticed he was still using the chicken nugget nickname."

Gideon snorted. "Except now it's chicky nuggy." He shook his head, more at himself. "I'm trying to decide if it still annoys me."

She chewed on the inside of her lip. "From your smile, I'm guessing it doesn't."

"I'll take all the wins where I can get them."

Lauren ate some of her lunch. Then, as if she was discussing the weather, she added, "He's cute too, don't you think?"

He met her gaze. "No. I mean, sure. He's . . . whatever. But that cannot happen. Don't even go there. I'm not interested. Not in anything to do with another man. Probably ever. And certainly not with a guy who's basically come into my life like a saving grace."

Lauren put her hand up. "I was just stating an observation."

Gideon stopped himself from saying anything else. 'Maybe the man doth protest too much' rang in his head, so he said nothing else. Because he knew Toby was cute. He knew Toby was sweet and funny and so wonderful with Benson.

And yes, he'd caught himself staring a time or two. He knew this too. But he was still incredibly heartsore. Drew had left a gaping wound on Gideon's heart he doubted would ever heal, and Toby was an angel who'd come to help. Nothing more.

Nothing more.

———

THE FIRST TWO WEEKS FLEW BY.

It wasn't exactly hard to get used to, Toby admitted. Beautiful house, beautiful baby, beautiful weather. He'd missed the sunshine after three years in England. Sydney's spring weather was absolutely perfect.

He'd missed his family, especially his brother and his parents too, but coming from an Italian family, there were a lot of relatives he hadn't seen in years. He'd missed his mum's cooking so much that a family BBQ in their backyard, with all his aunts and uncles and cousins, was a great way to spend his first Saturday off. Sharing a table on the back patio with them and a few beers had been the best way to spend a warm afternoon.

"First time off in two weeks," his uncle said. "That's a bit rough. Are your new bosses slave drivers or something?"

"No, not at all," Toby replied. "He's just a very new single dad, trying to work full-time and do everything after his partner walked out on them. You should have seen him. He was about to drop."

"Oh, I remember those days," his aunt added. "Just dreadful. And on his own? Poor guy."

Toby nodded. "I was supposed to have last weekend off, but honestly, we were just getting into a great routine and my boss had finally gotten some sleep, so I thought I'd stay on. There's always an adjustment period, so it was fine. And you should see this baby. Cutest kid you ever saw. Three months old, big eyes, big smile."

And you should see the dad . . .

"Tell them who your boss looks like," Josh said, his shit-eating grin in place, like he could read Toby's mind.

Toby rolled his eyes, but everyone waited for him to answer. "He may or may not look like Magnum PI. Well, he has a Tom Selleck moustache. The 1980s Magnum PI."

"Ooooh, hot," Gigi said, excitedly. Toby's older cousin had always been like a sister to him. "And he's single?"

Toby shook his head. "He's my boss."

"I'm not asking for you, pretty gay boy who can get anyone he wants," she said. "I'm talking about me, eternally single me. Who hasn't had a date in far too long."

They all laughed, and Toby sat back, loving every minute of his family's bantering and bickering, his mum trying to feed everyone until they exploded, his dad telling her to sit down and stop fussing.

He'd missed it all so much and he was so very happy to be home.

Even if he did catch himself checking the time and wondering if Benson was awake, if he'd had his bottle, if he'd gone down for his nap.

If Gideon was okay.

Toby knew Gideon was more than capable. He knew Gideon could cope just fine without him, especially now he'd managed to get some sleep. But Toby still found himself wondering. Worrying.

He wanted to text and ask a dozen times—maybe even call—but stopped himself. Gideon would have it all under control, and Benson would be fine. He'd managed six weeks on his own, more or less, before Toby arrived, he could certainly handle one weekend.

Even if Gideon was convinced he'd failed, he certainly hadn't. He'd done an outstanding job, and if Toby called maybe Gideon would think he wasn't capable.

So he didn't call or text.

Except on Sunday afternoon.

> I'll be back around six. Want me to pick up some dinner on my way?

He knew as soon as he'd sent it, Gideon would reply with something like 'that's not necessary, I don't expect you to do that' or some other kind of brush off.

So, before Gideon could reply, Toby sent another one.

> I'm getting us some Thai food. See you at six.

A little bossy, yes, but Toby had learned that Gideon

responded better to Toby making a quick decision, and he'd just go along with it. Otherwise, Gideon would stress over putting other people out and try to do everything himself.

Toby could see Gideon chose his battles well. He was too stressed and sleep deprived to sweat the small stuff.

So Thai dinner it was.

Toby let himself into the house just before six. There was no one in the front room, but he could hear a gentle singing down the hall and the splashing of water. Gideon was bathing Benson and singing to him. Not an actual song, just a happy nonsense tune, and it filled Toby with a happiness he wasn't quite expecting.

He stood there for a moment, just listening.

"It's just me," Toby called out gently, hating to interrupt them but not wanting to scare them.

A few seconds later, Gideon appeared, holding a freshly bathed Benson wrapped up in a towel. His dark hair was still damp, all chubby cheeks and huge smiles.

Toby pretended to tickle him. "Oh, look at this little one, all wrapped up like a chicky nuggy burrito."

Gideon sighed, but there was a hint of a smile. "Chicken nugget burrito?"

Toby grinned. "The cutest kind." He held up the Thai takeout. "Dinner is served."

"I'll just dress the burrito in his jarmies," Gideon said with a roll of his eyes.

That made Toby laugh as he grabbed some plates and set the table, and by the time he'd gotten two glasses of water, Gideon was putting Benson in his swing seat with his favourite caterpillar toy.

Toby took a seat and began to dish up the food. "I didn't know what you really liked, so I grabbed a few things and thought we'd just put it in the middle and pick at it. You can take the leftovers to work tomorrow if you want. Though I did ask for no coriander and to go light on the chili."

He looked up to see Gideon staring at him. He blinked himself out of wherever his thoughts had taken him. "It's perfect, thank you. And you didn't have to do this. I could have cooked something, or ordered in."

"I knew you'd say that," Toby said, taking a mouthful of the chicken. "Which is why I sent the second text saying I was doing it." He pointed his fork at the pad krapow gai. "That's really good."

Gideon smiled as he tasted it, nodding his agreement. "Have you ever been told you're kinda bossy?"

Toby grinned around a mouthful of rice. "All the time."

They ate a few bites in silence. "So," Gideon said. "Did you see your family?"

"All of them," Toby replied. "Aunts, uncles, cousins. My mum thought it would be good to shake the family tree so I could see everyone in one go. I come from a big Italian family. Very loud, lots of yelling and talking over each other, way too much food, and lots of love."

Gideon's eyes softened. "Sounds nice."

"What about you?" Toby asked. They hadn't really discussed families. They hadn't really discussed much besides Benson. "Big family?"

He shook his head. "My parents died when I was nine. My grandma took us in, not that she really wanted to, but anyway, she did. She wasn't thrilled at having two young kids to look after all over again. And she passed away about ten years ago now. So, it's just me and my sister, Benson's birth mum. We were never that close. Which sounds weird, considering I adopted her baby. But she was putting him up for adoption regardless of who adopted him. I have so little family that I . . ."

Toby smiled. "She made the choice that was right for her and for the baby."

He nodded with a sigh. "She moved to Melbourne pretty much straight after and asked for no updates or contact. Said it'd be easier for everyone. Maybe she's right. I don't know."

"That can't have been easy on anyone." Toby felt bad for asking, his dinner now not so appealing. "Wow. I'm . . ." Toby wasn't sure what to say. "Sorry."

Gideon ate some of the panang curry and used a serviette to wipe his moustache. "We weren't close, even as kids. I was older, and losing our parents was hard on everyone. We didn't dislike each other. We just weren't close. And when I was at uni, I kept in touch and sent her some money. But she was a moody teenager, got into trouble, that kind of thing. I left uni and got a job in the city, whereas she finished high school and bailed."

Jeez.

Toby couldn't even imagine what that was like. He was third generation Italian Australian, and family was everything. He decided to lighten the mood. "And now you've got your own family." He nodded to where Benson was babbling to the caterpillar, kicking his little legs.

Gideon smiled as he watched him. "I do. Just me and him."

"Army of two. You can take on the world."

"Well, two weeks ago I would have laughed at that. Or cried. But I'm feeling better about things now. Maybe my little army of two could take on getting to the park." His smile turned sad. "God, two weeks ago, I couldn't even do that."

"Did you get to the park this weekend?"

He made a face. "No. I did push the pram around the

block, and I took him around the backyard a few times, showed him the trees. I think he likes the greenery."

"That's really great!"

"It's not the park."

"It doesn't have to be. You have a backyard." Admittedly, it was kind of small, but it may as well have been Hyde Park compared to the London flats Toby had lived in that hadn't even had a balcony. "I don't think Benson knows the difference yet. Just wait until he discovers swings and climbing frames. Then you'll be going to the park."

Gideon granted him a smile. "You're a natural at this."

"Ah. It started with the big family and looking after baby cousins. I was all of eight years old and put in charge of a battalion of toddlers."

He laughed. "Nothing fazes you."

Toby shrugged as he ate more chicken and rice. "I'll tell you something, and I don't mean this to sound rude or ungrateful, but this is my job." Gideon flinched, and Toby was quick to amend what he'd said. "Don't misunderstand. Let me put it this way: what do you have at your job? Finances, clients, portfolios, markets, interest rates, stuff I can't even begin to understand. And then you also have all of this." He gestured to the room. "Your house, the mortgage, the bills. And on top of that, a considerable portion of your brain is now dedicated to worrying about Benson. Every second of every minute of every day. You have all of that going on, and you know what I have going on?"

Gideon shrugged.

"Benson," Toby said. "Just him. Okay, and maybe you, somewhat. But mostly Benson. That's all. Making sure he's fed and happy. I mean, there's more to it than that, obviously. But you get my point. This is all I do. If I don't do laundry one day, what's the worst that could happen?" He sipped his water. "You've got a dozen balls in the air at any given time, and I'm over here reading *A Very Hungry Caterpillar* and singing 'Twinkle, Twinkle Little Star.'"

Gideon stared at him.

"Maybe give yourself a break," Toby offered gently. "You're doing a wonderful job. And I'll tell you another trade secret, and this one's a doozy."

"What's that?"

"No parent knows what they're doing. Not one." Toby met his gaze. "Not even parents with five or six kids. They might get the hang of some things, but then a curve ball comes along and the wheels fall off. There's no instruction manual, and every child is different. All the self-help books in the world can't tell you what it's really like." Gideon didn't look convinced. "I'm telling you," Toby added, "it's true."

"So what are you saying? That everyone is just winging it? Not just me?"

Toby chuckled. "Every single parent. You can ask ten different parents for advice and you'll likely get ten different answers. Sure, some people seem to have their shit together, but I can guarantee you it's not always like that. As soon as something new happens, they're straight on the phone to someone being like 'help, what do I do?'."

Gideon was quiet for a moment. "I don't have anyone I can really ask anything. Google is a minefield, but some parenting sites are okay. I've been treating that *What to Expect* book like a bible."

"And that's perfect. Not everyone has the support network of family to rely on. So really, can you see just how well you've done so far?"

His lips twitched under that gorgeous moustache, but

he didn't say anything. It was very clear Gideon didn't take compliments very well.

"And now you have me," Toby added cheerfully in an attempt to lighten the mood. "You're both your little army of two, and I'm more the backup, reinforcement guy. A wingman with the nappy bag, if you will."

He smiled and picked at some rice with his fork. "So, do you really sing 'Twinkle, Twinkle Little Star' to him?"

"Yes," Toby replied in the tone of *duhhh*. "He loves my singing voice. Thinks it's very funny."

Gideon's smile was so carefree, and Toby caught a glimpse of the man Gideon was before he became so guarded.

Chapter Five

GIDEON WASN'T SURE HOW IT HAPPENED, BUT BEFORE he knew it, Benson was five months old. Twenty-two weeks. Sixteen weeks since Drew walked out on them. Ten weeks since Toby moved in and changed everything.

Gideon had secured more contracts at work, and not just because he was sleeping better. He *was* eating better, getting more fresh air, and having more structure and less stress.

All because of Toby.

Toby cooked dinner most nights, took care of most of the laundry, and cleaned and tidied up, which left Gideon's time with Benson purely Dadda-and-son time.

He still FaceTimed him every day at one o'clock, and it was still Gideon's favourite time of day—seeing those chubby cheeks and gummy smiles fill the screen on his phone. Then he got to come home, have playtime, feed and bathe him, have cuddles, and put him to bed.

Benson was thriving. He was happy, growing like a weed, passing every milestone at a rate of knots.

Toby had been a godsend.

Most nights they ate dinner together and Toby would relay everything that happened that day, appointments they'd had, or their trips to the park where he'd inadvertently met a bunch of other mums and nannies and, weather permitting, they'd catch up a few times a week.

Sometimes they even watched TV together. Some nights, if Gideon had work to catch up on, Toby would read a book in his room, but most nights they'd watch *Drag Race* or *Great British Bake Off* reruns together.

Gideon liked those nights best.

Toby would make them a cup of hot raspberry tea with a square of dark chocolate on the side to cap off the day. They'd sit on separate sofas, and Gideon would sometimes catch himself glancing at Toby.

All sat up with a leg tucked under himself, he'd laugh at something on telly, his cup of tea in hand. Or he'd shake his head at the utter gall of a cooking contestant not knowing they should have proved the bread a second time . . .

A few times more than he'd like to admit, Gideon had to make himself look away. He didn't want Toby.

He wanted to not be lonely.

He wanted this—how easy this was—with the life he was supposed to have with Drew.

He wanted Benson to have his two dads.

He wanted a lot of things, but his life had taken a sharp detour sixteen weeks ago. Then ten weeks ago the road smoothed out a bit, and he'd been coasting so comfortably the last month or so, he hadn't even realised . . .

He wasn't lonely anymore.

He had Toby. And even though their relationship was strictly professional, maybe Toby was getting Gideon through the grief of the death of his relationship. Maybe

Toby didn't even know, but having him around helped Gideon more than he'd realised.

Gideon hadn't thought of Drew in a few days, a week even.

And that was a first.

"Oh, for real. How is that guy an amateur baker," Toby said, nodding to the TV. "Look at how good that is."

Gideon found himself smiling. "I don't know how they do half of what they do. I struggle to make toast."

"I know." Then Toby's gaze shot to Gideon's. "I mean, the toast you make is great."

"I like it cooked."

He nodded behind his cup of tea. "Charcoal's good for your teeth, apparently."

Gideon laughed at that. "Burnt toast with peanut butter is my guilty pleasure."

Toby finished his tea and stood up, his hand out for Gideon's cup. "I'm going to get ready for bed. I'll take the nightshift tonight."

"Are you sure?"

"Yeah. Didn't you say you've got an early meeting tomorrow?"

"Well, yes, but—"

"Then it's fine." He put the cups into the sink, and when he walked past, he lightly squeezed Gideon's arm. "See you in the morning."

Gideon's arm burned where Toby had touched him, warmth lingering.

Toby's bedroom door closed with a quiet snick and Gideon stood there for a few uncertain seconds before he turned the light off and went to his room. He needed to get this nonsense out of his head. He needed to stop thinking of Toby in any way that was inappropriate.

And it wasn't that Gideon wanted anything sexual with Toby. He just felt at ease; he felt comfort around him. He trusted him with Benson, and there was a profound weight to that.

Gideon needed to stop catching glances at him. He needed to *not* like the sound of Toby's laughter, and he needed to stop being lonely and desperate for human connection and to start treating Toby in a manner he deserved.

Professional.

After all, Toby had said this was just a job to him. It was, in his words, his job to look after both of them.

And maybe that realisation, that Toby was only being nice to him because it was his job, maybe that smarted a little. It certainly made his loneliness ache a whole lot more.

Get yourself together, Gideon.

What he needed was his friends. He sat down on the edge of his bed and plugged his phone in to charge but shot a quick text off to Lauren. He hadn't seen them in over a week, which was almost a record.

> Miss you guys. Lunch at my place on Saturday?

Lauren's reply came through immediately.

> Can't do Saturday. Jill's dad's birthday. What about Sunday lunch?

Gideon knew that Toby would be at his parent's place until six. He thumbed out a reply.

> Perfect.

He put his phone down, stood up, and pulled his shirt

off, heading toward his en suite. He had his pants unbuttoned and was just about to pull them down when he heard Benson fussing.

It was too early for a bottle. And Gideon was pretty sure Toby was in the shower; he said he was getting ready for bed. Then Benson cried and Gideon rushed for the door, pulling it open, and almost ran smack bang into Toby.

Freshly showered, clean PJs, damp hair. "Oh," Toby said, his hand to his heart. "You startled me."

"Sorry, I—"

Toby's eyes went to Gideon's chest, then lower, lower . . .

And Gideon realised his pants were undone. He quickly buttoned them up. "Oh shit, sorry. Was heading to the shower."

Benson wailed and Toby's attention went to the closed door. "I'll get him."

He went in, keeping the lights off, his voice low. "What's wrong, my little chicky nuggy?" he murmured. Benson stopped crying when Toby picked him up. "Oh wow. Nappy change required, *stat*."

Gideon stood there in the hallway, out of view, listening to them. Smiling.

"To the moon and back," Toby said. "I bet they could smell this on the moon." Gideon heard the Velcro nappy tabs. "Oh jeez." And then Toby gagged loudly, and Benson giggled.

Gideon had to bite back a laugh.

"Holy dooly." Toby gasped. "Is this a teething poop? I think it might be. Is my little chicken nugget getting a tooth?"

Gideon didn't even know teething poops were a thing.

"Pants back on, and I think I might try for a bottle now

and see if a certain little man sleeps till breakfast," Toby said, and Gideon knew he was saying this out loud for his benefit. To make himself scarce, because if Benson saw him in the hallway, no one was going back to bed for a while.

He quietly slipped into his room, pulling the door closed behind him as quietly as possible.

He took a quick shower and climbed into bed. He set his alarm, turned his bedside light off, and smiled into the darkness.

⸻

"What do you mean he saw you shirtless with your pants undone?"

"I was getting undressed to have a shower," Gideon explained. They'd finished lunch some time ago and were sitting around talking. Both Jill and Lauren were staring at him. Benson was on Lauren's lap, a teething ring in his mouth.

"And?"

"And he . . . he looked."

"Did he say anything?"

"Nope. Never mentioned it." Gideon eyed them both. "And neither did I. Which is a good thing. That's not what this is."

"But . . . ?" Jill pushed.

"But nothing." Gideon was not admitting anything.

Jill stared at him. "Gideon," she said softly. "I've known you a very long time."

He sighed. "Look. He's great. He's smart and funny, and he's sooooo good with Benson. But he's employed by me, and that makes it weird, and gross. Not to mention that I am wholly sworn off men for all eternity."

"Same," Lauren added with a very lesbian smirk.

Gideon looked at Jill. "I would never risk or jeopardise what I have with him. He's the best nanny ever. He quite literally saved my life. And Benson's. God knows what would've happened if he wasn't here. I depend on him for far too much as it is."

Jill patted his arm. "All I'm saying is that you and Toby already have things you do together."

He squinted at her. "What do you mean?"

"Things you do . . . together. He gets takeaway for dinner on a Sunday. It's a thing you do. You have favourite TV shows you watch together. It's a thing you do. He makes you cups of tea before bed. It's a thing you do."

"It's his job," Gideon said lamely. He wasn't even sure he believed it.

Jill shook her head, and when Gideon looked at Lauren, she shook her head too. "That's not his job."

Gideon knew it wasn't in Toby's job description to watch TV with him or to make him cups of tea.

Goddammit.

"I'm not lonely with him here," Gideon whispered. "He's filled a void in my life. A very platonic void. You know I need to be around people, I always have, and he's great company. I don't need anything more than that. I don't want anything more than that. After Drew . . ." Gideon shook his head. "It's just me and Benson now. And while I'm going through all this and while Benson's so dependent, Toby fills the void. Platonically. And that sounds bad, I know. But I'm paying him and it's his job, and if I get to not be lonely because we watch TV sometimes, then is that so terrible?"

Jill frowned and shook her head. "No. It's not terrible." She put her arm around Gideon's shoulder and gave him a hug. "I'm sorry. Now tell me again about this little guy. Is he really getting a tooth?"

He shrugged and gave a nod. "Toby said they can go up and down for a few weeks before they break the gum."

"Ouch!" Lauren kissed Benson's head. "Poor little chicky nuggy."

Gideon sighed at the name, but the three of them looked at each other and smiled.

A short while later, Gideon's phone rang. It was face up on the table and he stopped dead when he saw the name of the caller.

Drew.

His heart rate shot through the roof, his stomach rolled, and he felt cold all over.

What the hell?

"Don't answer it," Jill said sharply, her eyes going from the screen to Gideon. "Do not answer it."

TOBY GOT BACK TO THE HOUSE JUST BEFORE SIX, LIKE he did every Sunday, with a bag of takeout in his hand. He was in such a good mood. He'd had a great weekend hanging out with his brother, but he was really looking forward to seeing Benson. He missed the little cherub, even having only been gone two days.

And Gideon.

He'd missed him too. Which was absurd. But his smile, the way his eyes squinted when he laughed, and his ridiculously gorgeous moustache.

Just as he was about to put his key in the door, it opened, and Lauren held the door for him. She wasn't smiling. "Come in."

"What's wrong?" he whispered, fear ratcheting upwards. "Is Benson okay?"

Jill appeared from the kitchen holding Benson, a worried look on her face. "He's fine, but . . ."

And then Gideon came from the hallway, staggering and incredibly drunk.

"Oh."

"Hey," Gideon said, his smile crooked, his stance lopsided too. Jesus, how much had he had to drink? "'Dja bring food?"

Toby looked at the takeout bag he was holding. "Uh yeah. Greek lamb and potatoes."

Lauren took it with pleading eyes. "Food is probably a good idea."

He nodded, because yes, it was probably a great idea.

Gideon followed Lauren into the kitchen and Jill went to Toby. "God, Toby," she whispered. "I'm so sorry. Drew called."

"He did?"

Holy shit. Toby wasn't sure why that shocked him. And stung, if he was being honest.

He put his hands out to Benson and Benson leaned toward him, wanting to go to him, and Toby felt instant relief as soon as he was holding him. "Well, I'd ask if he's okay, but clearly he's not."

Jill shook her head. "I told him not to answer it. That asshole can scream into the abyss for all I care."

"Do you know what was said?"

She shook her head. "He took his phone and answered it in the backyard. He was out there for maybe two minutes. Came back in and opened the bottle of Scotch they got for some anniversary gift. He guzzled half of it before I took it off him. He's not a big drinker, Toby. He hasn't ever done this before, but he was really upset and angry. I'm sorry." She took little Benson's hand. "If you want us to stay, we'll stay."

Toby found himself rocking from one foot to the other, and he kissed the side of Benson's head. "No, it'll be fine. I think Dadda might be asleep before Benson tonight."

She nodded. "God, what a mess. You have my number. Call if you need anything. He's a placid drunk—usually just dances and sings badly, laughs at everything. But he was pretty upset."

"Then he dove headfirst into a bottle of Scotch."

"And it wasn't a cheap bottle, and it was high proof."

Which would explain his level of intoxication.

Lauren appeared. "He's eating, at least. It's not pretty, but it should help."

Toby didn't know what the hell Drew could have said that made Gideon react this way. The truth was, Gideon very rarely spoke of Drew, and when he did, it was with a hint of disdain. Toby had never asked for any more details than he did on that first day. He'd needed to know if there was any custody or visitation requirements and . . .

Oh no.

A cold and dreadful feeling settled in Toby's gut. "Do you think it was about visitation or custody?"

Jill and Lauren stared at him. Jill's nostrils flared and fire flashed in her eyes. "It wouldn't fucking want to be," she murmured.

Lauren shook her head. "Surely not. He walked away months ago, when Benson was just a few weeks old. He wanted nothing to do with him. Why would he want anything now?"

Toby kissed Benson's temple again, holding him a little tighter. There was a whole list of reasons, and none of them were good—so he didn't have to pay child support. To hurt Gideon. For no other reason than because he could.

Not that he said any of this out loud.

Toby had never even laid eyes on Drew. But lord, how he despised him.

A chair scraped on the kitchen floor and Gideon mumbled, "Where is everybody?"

Then he appeared, swaying, sauce of some kind on his cheek but somehow not in his moustache. He saw Toby holding Benson and he rocked back. "Look at you. My baby boy," he said, his eyes now filled with tears. "You ever love someone so much?" But then he swayed too far left and Lauren helped grab him. He put his hands up. "Sorry. Sorry. Wanna hold my baby boy but—" He shook his head and wiped at his eye. "Fuck, I'm drunk. Sorry."

"How about we get you into bed?" Lauren said.

Gideon nodded and swayed again, his eyes still glassy. He scrubbed his hand over his face, his gaze landing on Toby. "Thank you. I'm sorry. I'll do the night shift," he slurred.

There was no way Gideon was doing anything of the sort.

He reached for Benson's hand, frowning again, eyes wet. "To the moon and back," he mumbled.

Lauren led him to his room, and when he was gone, Jill sighed. She gave Toby a sad smile. "Please don't think bad of him. I don't think he even allowed himself to cry when Drew left. He had to be the strong one for Benson. Believe me, he'll feel bad enough for everyone tomorrow."

Toby wasn't sure what to say to that. He didn't think bad of him at all.

He felt sorry for him.

But Benson began to fuss, so Toby got him a bottle

while Jill cleaned up the mess Gideon had made of dinner. Lauren came back out looking somewhat dismayed. "I put a bucket beside his bed."

Toby snorted. "Nice."

"Better than puke on the floor."

"So true."

"He was trying not to cry," she whispered.

Jill sagged. "I'll go sit with him for a bit, then we can go." Lauren gave her a smile and rubbed her arm as she went past.

Toby hated the thought of Gideon being upset but he didn't want Benson to pick up on that, so he hid his concern and smiled at Benson, who was having his bottle. "Hey, my little chicken nugget."

Benson smiled around the teat, and Toby grinned at him. "My *cheeky* little chicky nuggy."

Lauren rubbed Toby's arm. "He adores you."

"It's mutual," he replied. Toby had loved all the kids he'd cared for, but Benson was special.

Jill came back out, looking beat. "He's asleep."

"Is he okay?" Toby asked, sitting Benson upright so he could burp, rubbing his back.

"He's gonna be sick tomorrow." They collected their bags and gave Toby an apologetic smile. "Call us if you need anything. Any time of the night."

"Will do. Thanks."

Toby locked the door behind them, got Benson bathed and eventually put him to bed, then went out to the kitchen to finish tidying up. He picked at some of the Greek lamb, but he really didn't have much of an appetite.

It had been such a weird night. An eventful night, and educational. He'd learned that Gideon rarely ever drank—in his time there, Toby had never seen him drink—and he'd learned that Jill and Lauren were amazing. He'd met them several times and they'd always been lovely and great friends to Gideon, but they'd really helped out tonight.

And Toby learned that he felt things for Gideon that he wasn't prepared to feel. He cared for him. It pained Toby to see him hurting.

He wasn't sure what to make of any of that.

He stared at the TV for an hour or two, his mind reeling, until he made himself get up. He set the dishwasher going and turned the light off when Gideon appeared. "Need water," he mumbled. He wasn't swaying so much anymore, but his eyes were barely open.

"I'll get it for you." Toby filled a glass and handed it to him. "Are you okay?"

Gideon took a long drink, then shook his head. "I'm really sorry."

"It's okay, Gideon," Toby said gently.

He put the glass on the counter. "Benson asleep?"

"Yeah."

He frowned and his shoulders fell. "I'm sorry," he said again. "I'm his father and I let him down."

"No you didn't."

His gaze met Toby's. "I hate Drew so much. I hate him." A tear escaped his eye, not that he seemed to notice. "He wants out of the mortgage. Wants to sell or for me to buy him out. Which is fine. Actually, I'm glad. He stopped paying his share the day he moved out. But he saw his lawyer to make it all official, taking me out of his will and whatever. Wanna know why? So if something happens to me, he's not in any way responsible for Benson. Not that he would have been. But just to be sure. And it's not that he doesn't even want to have anything to do with Benson, but he *absolutely* doesn't want to fucking have anything to do with him." Gideon wiped his tears away. "How could he hate him so much? Benson's innocent in this and, ugh, it makes me so mad! You know what he said? He said he still loves me and he misses me, but he didn't want to be a dad. He said taking in my nephew ruined our relationship. He called him my nephew." His nose was running and tears streamed down his face as he sobbed. "Who the fuck says that? Benson's my son." He thumped his chest. "He's my son."

Toby swallowed back his own tears and he did what felt right. He pulled Gideon in for a hug. Gideon smelled of alcohol, but he was solid and heavy against him. And Toby wrapped his arms around him, holding him tight.

Gideon sobbed and cried, his hands fisting the back of Toby's shirt. "I hate him," he mumbled through his tears. "I hate him so much."

Toby held him tight, wondering when the last time Gideon had been hugged or held, or had any kind of human touch other than when he held his son. From the way he was clinging to Toby, he'd guess it had probably been a while.

And they stood there in the kitchen until Gideon was all cried out. He was heavy against Toby, who wondered if he'd fallen asleep. Toby rubbed his back. "You okay?"

He shook his head. "No."

Then Gideon's forehead pressed to Toby's neck, then his jaw, then his cheek, his breaths short and sharp, his hands still fisting in Toby's shirt.

Toby's heart was stuttering.

Their mouths were so close.

So close.

Almost a kiss.

But then Gideon's face crumpled and he pulled away.

49

He took an unsteady step back, keeping his head down. "Sorry. Fuck, I'm sorry." He took another step back and turned away, his hand to his forehead. "I'm sorry."

Before Toby could answer, Gideon was gone.

Toby slumped against the counter and let out a few deep breaths. What the hell had just happened?

Was Gideon about to kiss him?

Did Toby want him to?

No, of course not . . .

Maybe.

Just a little bit.

He'd be lying if he said he hadn't thought about it, if he said he didn't find Gideon insanely attractive.

But he was also his boss and Toby was living in his house, and as if that wasn't complicated enough, Gideon was drunk.

He just needed a friend.

Toby refilled the glass of water, found some headache pills, and intended to put them on Gideon's bedside table, but when he poked his head into Gideon's room, his bed was empty. The door to the en suite bathroom was ajar, the light off. He wasn't in there.

And when he peeked into Benson's room, sure enough, Gideon was folded up on the small sofa next to the crib, sound asleep.

Clearly Gideon felt guilty for not being in any state to look after Benson and needed to be close to him.

How could Toby be mad at him?

He wasn't angry that Gideon got drunk. He wasn't mad or even disappointed. He felt bad for him; he sympathised with him. He commiserated with him because Gideon's ex was an asshole. Benson wasn't his nephew. Drew would have said that for one purpose of hurting Gideon, and boy, did it work.

Toby wanted to protect them both.

He felt things for Gideon he rightly shouldn't feel.

And seeing him squeezed onto the tiny sofa just to be close to Benson wasn't helping.

Toby put the water and Panadol on Gideon's bedside table, pulled the throw blanket from Gideon's bed and gently laid it over him. His back and neck were going to be hell tomorrow, not to mention the headache he'd most definitely have.

Toby guessed none of that would come close to how heartsore he'd be.

Chapter Six

GIDEON WOKE UP ON THE FLOOR IN BENSON'S ROOM.
He had a vague recollection of sitting on the sofa and
resting his head. He'd just wanted a few minutes to listen to
Benson breathe . . .

He tried to sit up and regretted it immediately. Everything hurt. His back felt like a stack of pebbles, and his
head . . . wow.

It'd been so long since his last hangover, he couldn't
remember them being this bad.

Benson's crib was empty, and the brightened edge to the
blinds told him it was morning.

Monday morning.

Christ, he had to go to work.

He had no recollection of how he'd ended up on the
floor, and no recollection of how the blanket off his bed was
now tangled around his hips, unless Toby had . . .

Shit.

Toby.

Gideon had flashbacks of losing his shit in the kitchen

and of Toby holding him, his arms strong, his body so warm . . .

Or was that a dream?

Then he remembered telling him what Drew had said to him over the phone. How he'd got upset all over again, how he couldn't stop the tears.

How Toby had hugged him, comforted him.

How Gideon had almost kissed him.

"Oh god."

Gideon scrubbed his hands over his face and got to his feet, his body protesting every inch of the way. But his head . . . It wasn't pounding, per se. It just felt like an axe was lodged in his brain.

And then his stomach decided to join the pity party.

But he needed to check on Benson.

He got to the hall, determined to not let the brightness of the lounge room deter him.

"Good morning," Toby said. He was sitting on the couch with Benson on his knee, burping him, an empty bottle beside them.

Benson smiled when he saw him.

"Morning," he replied.

"How're you feeling?"

Gideon shook his head. "What time is it?"

"Almost seven."

He cringed and slumped himself onto the sofa beside them. Toby propped Benson up on Gideon's lap and stood. "This little guy was starving. He had a big bottle this morning."

"Like Dadda yesterday."

Toby snorted. "I'll make some coffee."

Gideon wrapped Benson up in a hug and inhaled that familiar baby smell, and Benson rewarded him with a huge burp. Gideon chuckled and bounced him on his knee, Benson's chubby little hands grabbing Gideon's moustache. Benson always grabbed at it, and it didn't hurt that bad.

Plus, Gideon didn't care too much right then and there. He pretty much hurt all over, and seeing Benson's big, drooly smile and bright blue eyes made everything better.

Toby came out from the kitchen holding a glass of fizzing Berocca. "Have this first." He took Benson. Gideon took the drink and downed it. It was never great, but he knew it would help.

Toby put Benson under his play gym and came back from the kitchen with two coffees.

"Thank you," Gideon said. He didn't want things to be awkward between them and knew he'd have to address what he'd done.

Toby sat, sipping his coffee, and even in his pyjamas with sleep-messed hair, he looked a whole lot better put together than how Gideon felt. And he waited for Gideon to speak.

"So," Gideon began, "about last night. I'm really sorry. I don't normally drink, and I know that's not an excuse. I want you to know that I won't be drinking again. And if I made you feel uncomfortable in any way, I am really sorry. You have every right to be pissed at me. It was inexcusable. And thank you for looking after Benson. I was in no shape to, and you totally stepped up when I failed." He frowned. "If you weren't here . . ."

"If I weren't here, Lauren and Jill would have stayed," Toby said. "I accept your apology, though you may want to call Jill and Lauren and offer them the same courtesy."

Gideon winced again. "You're right. I will."

"They were very worried."

He nodded. "I just . . . I just lost my shit. I held it

together for months, tried to be the strong one because I had to be." He looked at Benson, happily babbling and kicking at his play gym. "Then Drew kept calling him my nephew. Like I'm not a valid father. And I lost it."

Toby sighed. "I've never met Drew, and this is probably out of line, but I really don't like him." He met Gideon's eyes. "You are a father. You're Benson's dad, and you're a great dad. So you dropped the ball one time. I think that's allowed, considering everything you've been through. And Benson is absolutely fine."

"If it was just me and Benson here, or if you or anyone else weren't here, I'd never drink," Gideon said. "All the times it was just me and him alone here, I never drank. Not even a glass of wine."

"Well, I'm glad to hear that. I'd like to not have a repeat of last night, if I'm being honest."

Gideon nodded. Was that in regard to the drinking? Or to the hug? Gideon wasn't sure. He wasn't game to ask.

Toby sipped his coffee and chewed on his bottom lip. "If you need to talk or vent, or if you need a shoulder to cry on, I'm okay with that," he said quietly.

So, was that about the hug?

Gideon assumed it was but wasn't sure, so he nodded. "Thank you. I don't really have anyone . . . I had friends. I think Drew got them in the split. My entire life is right there." He nodded toward Benson. "Well, I have Lauren and Jill, of course, but I leaned on them a lot when Benson arrived, and then when Drew left, and . . ." He shrugged. "I was trying to spare them."

"I'm sure they'd want you to share your troubles, Gideon." He smiled but looked at the clock. "Are you going to work today?"

Gideon sighed. "Yeah."

Among other things he needed to do today, such as calling his solicitor and his banker, he did need to go to work. He'd never used a hangover as an excuse to not go to work. He took a mouthful of coffee. "Better get showered." He stood up, and even after all he'd said, he still felt as if it wasn't enough. "Thank you, Toby. For yesterday, and for everything as well. I'd be lost without you. And I know I was pretty drunk last night, but did we hug? Or did I dream that whole thing?"

Toby chuckled. "We did. In the kitchen."

"I thought so." He sagged. "Again, I'm really sorry. I just . . ."

"You needed a hug," Toby said. He smiled behind his coffee, but his eyes were soft. "It was fine. You'd had a shit day and you needed to vent and let off some steam. It was fine, Gideon."

"It was inappropriate of me, and I don't want you to think—"

"If it was inappropriate or non-consensual, I'd tell you. Or I'd have just kneed you in the nuts last night."

Gideon snorted. "Right. That's fair."

Benson started to whinge, and Toby put his coffee down and picked him up. "We need to get this little chicky nuggy out of these jarmies," he said as they disappeared down the hall.

Gideon took both coffee cups to the sink, then got himself showered and dressed for work, and was feeling half-human by the time he walked back into the lounge room. Benson was now having some tummy time on his blanket, chewing on his caterpillar, and Gideon wished he could stay home . . .

Toby came out from the kitchen with a plate of toast.

He took one look at Gideon and stopped. "Still not feeling good?"

"No, I'm okay," he mumbled. "Feeling much better after a shower."

"Here," Toby said, handing him a piece of toast. "It's not burnt to charcoal, which is apparently your favourite, but it will get you through the morning."

Gideon took it with a smile. "Thanks. Um, I don't know what time I'll be home. I need to try and see my solicitor and my banker today. About getting things changed with the house and whatnot."

"That's okay. Take as long as you need. We have a full day of laundry, maybe a trip to the supermarket, and a playdate in the park this afternoon, depending on how long someone naps for today. And if I'm lucky, maybe I'll get the vacuuming done."

Gideon groaned at how good that sounded compared to what he had to do. "Wanna swap?"

Toby shook his head. "One hundred percent no."

"Understandable." Gideon smiled, kissed Benson's forehead, and went to work.

TOBY WASN'T SURE IF HE SHOULD BRING UP THE HUG-almost-kiss that happened the night before, but he was glad Gideon had.

Not that he mentioned the almost-kiss. But he did acknowledge the hug, and he apologised a dozen times, not that Toby was even mad. When Toby had gone into Benson's room in the morning, Gideon was still on the floor next to the crib, sound asleep.

Because he wanted to be close to his son.

Toby couldn't be mad at him.

And maybe the hug had been somewhat inappropriate, but when Toby replayed it in his mind, he was pretty sure he had pulled Gideon in for a hug, not the other way around.

But the whole incident was over with, and the almost-kiss was forgotten.

Well, it would be forgotten if Toby could stop thinking about it.

At around one o'clock, Toby managed to get to the park for the playdate. It was just a local, informal gathering of parents and carers that met at the park on Mondays and Thursdays. Toby was the only guy, but not the only nanny. He had met one of the dads one time, though mostly it was between three and five adults and between three and seven or eight children, ranging in ages from five months to three years.

Benson was the youngest, but Malek was close at seven months. It was good to have another baby close in age, so while the other kids played and carers chased after them, Toby and Benson could sit on the blankets with Malek and his mum, Anika.

Toby was closer with Anika than any of the others that came along. Not close by any means, but they knew enough about each other to engage in conversation. She knew he'd been overseas for three years, that he had family in Sydney, and that Benson was the only child to a single dad.

Anika was on maternity leave with her third child. She was funny and said whatever was on her mind. Maybe she was a little uncouth, but it was part of her charm. Toby liked her the second they met.

Anika was maybe thirty-five and married to a wonderful man named Sean who, according to Anika, was the ringleader of their crazy circus. Their eldest was five, a girl called Anya, who was in kindergarten. The middle child was Riley, a two-year old boy who ran wild in the park, and little Malek was the cutest baby, with so much dark hair and the biggest brown eyes Toby had ever seen.

Anika made parenting three kids look easy, and she always made Toby's trip to the park more fun. Sometimes they gossiped about celebrities and TV shows, but mostly their conversations centred on the kids, feeding schedules, teething, and which supermarkets had the best sales that week.

After the day Toby'd had, the warm weather was lovely, the shade of the huge trees and the fresh air was everything he needed. And Benson loved it.

"You look like you had a rough weekend," Anika said.

"My weekend was great," he replied. "Last night was . . . weird. I didn't sleep much."

"Oh, that's not good," she whispered.

"It wasn't bad. But it wasn't great, either. Eye-opening and sad, mostly."

She frowned with a sigh. "With Benson's dad? Is everything okay?"

"Oh, sure," Toby said. "We cleared the air this morning, and everything is fine. I think I understand him better now."

"Is it weird, just the two of you? What happens when he gets home? Does he take over and you clock off?"

Toby shrugged. "Depends what he has on. He's very hands-on. He works a lot, but he dotes on Benson."

"And a single dad," she mused. "Can't be easy."

"No, he hasn't had it easy, that's for sure."

Anika gave Malek a teething rusk and wiped his chin. "He's lucky he can afford you," she said. There was no ill-intent to her words. As a nanny, Toby understood that the people who could afford to pay for full-time at-home carers were privileged. There were plenty of folks who couldn't afford care, and many had no family or friends to help.

But something about that had been playing on Toby's mind.

Gideon had mentioned having to buy his ex out of the house and take the mortgage on by himself. Either that or sell the house.

Or get rid of Toby.

What alternative care for Benson Gideon would get, Toby had no clue.

That thought didn't sit well with Toby.

He wasn't ready for his time with them to be up.

Benson fussed a little, so Toby sat him up, holding onto his hands. He wasn't sitting up on his own yet, though he was close. Then Toby stood him up, holding him but letting his legs bounce on the blanket. He squealed and babbled, much happier.

"Such a cutie!" Anika said, giving Benson's tummy a little tickle. Then, after a few seconds, she said, "Mm, speaking of cuties." She pointed her chin over Toby's shoulder. "Oh jeez, he's coming this way. Do we know this guy?"

Toby looked.

Holy shit.

"Uh, yes. We sure do." Toby turned Benson around so he could see. "Can you see your dadda?"

Anika nudged him and hissed, "You never said he was hot."

Gideon was wearing his grey suit pants, white shirt—tucked in, of course—and yes, his sleeves were now rolled up his forearms. It didn't hurt that the pants were well-fitted, that his shirt was tailored perfectly for his body.

It didn't hurt at all.

"Do you mind if I join you?" Gideon asked.

"Of course not," Toby said. "Take a seat. Look, Benson. Look who it is."

Gideon sat on the blanket, and as soon as Benson saw him, he squealed and put out his little hands for him. Gideon grinned as he took him, giving him a quick hug and smooch on his chubby cheek before sitting him up in his lap.

Toby made quick introductions to the others, adults and kids, and Gideon smiled, although there was a weariness in his eyes, in his smile.

Toby knew Gideon had some important things going on today but didn't want to bring them up in front of the others.

"I was going home," Gideon volunteered, as if he'd read Toby's mind. "Was driving past and saw you so I doubled back." He kissed the top of Benson's head. "Thought a sit in the park with my favourite little man sounded perfect."

"Well, you made this one happy," Toby said, giving Benson a little goose on the leg. He was babbling and gurgling, one fist shoved in his mouth, drooling everywhere, and Toby wiped Benson's chin with his bib.

One of the other kids cried after taking a spill on the grass. Another one cried because they wanted more watermelon when what they really needed was a nap. And thus began the inevitable packing up. One mum began to pack up because she had to pick kids up from school, and Anika did the same. Toby helped her with Malek while she chased after Riley and packed up their things, grateful she didn't have far to walk to the school to get Anya. Another carer needed to be home in time for the older kids to get off the bus, and someone else needed to go to the supermarket.

Soon enough, it was just Toby, Gideon, and Benson.

"Did me turning up cause a mass exodus?" Gideon asked.

Toby chuckled. "No. It's nearly three o'clock; that means school's almost out. And the afternoon meet-up on Mondays are tricky. Mornings are usually better because all the kids aren't tired. In the afternoon, you never know what you're gonna get. But it's good timing for the afternoon school run."

"Guess I have all that to look forward to."

"Yes, you do." He was almost afraid to ask, but now was as a good time as any. "You left work early today?"

Gideon nodded. "I was useless this morning. Me and hangovers do not mix. I did what needed doing and my boss told me to call it a day. And I spoke to my solicitor's office. Well, I spoke to an associate. Long story short, it's just a matter of amending paperwork, which is good. Plus the amendments to my will, removing Drew from everything. They were drafting everything up and would get my solicitor to look at it and call me."

"That's good, right?"

He nodded. "Yeah. I should have done it before now. But then I called my banker and ran some numbers. Being in corporate finance, I should know all this, but it's overwhelming when it's aimed at you. Anyway, he was really good about everything. It means a total overhaul, refinancing, cashing stocks to cover . . ." He seemed to catch himself, as if he was probably sharing too much. "Anyway, all that's in my name. Drew and I almost bought stocks together. Thank god I kept it separate. But my banker knew what to do—I guess he deals with separations all the time."

Toby sighed and rubbed Gideon's arm. "It can't have been easy."

Gideon sighed and shook his head. "Actually, I feel

good about it now. Once he talked me through it, I could see that at first it was about Drew wanting to protect himself, but now it's about me protecting me and Benson. I really should have done it sooner."

"You've been kinda busy," Toby allowed.

Gideon shrugged. "I should have made time. I'm in finance, albeit corporate insurance. Not exactly the same, but I should have known better." He picked Benson up and blew raspberries on his cheek. "I'll be paying off my mortgage until I'm one hundred and sixty years old. But it's all mine. Well, it will be."

Toby chuckled, but then he thought of something . . . "Will you need to cut my hours? To cut expenses? Not that I want that to happen." The thought made him feel awful. "It'd be understandable."

Gideon scoffed. "God, no. If anything, I need to work more so I can make the mortgage payments, so I can keep the house; for me to work longer hours, I need you more than ever. My boss is fine with some remote work, but a lot of what I do has to be done in the office. There are files and confidential information, that kind of thing. I'll try to not be away from home more, but Toby, you've been a life saver! I couldn't cut your hours, I would be absolutely lost without you."

Toby felt a rush of warmth at his words. "Well, life saver might be a stretch. Sanity saver, maybe."

He grinned at that. "Life and sanity. Both. And as another apology for last night, I thought I'd cook dinner tonight. If you're okay with that?"

Toby couldn't hide his surprise. "Uh, sure!"

"And one more thing."

"What's that?"

"Please don't ever let me sleep on the floor again."

Toby laughed. "You *were* on the little sofa in Benson's room."

He groaned. "No wonder my back is killing me."

Benson started to grizzle, so Toby stood up. "Come on, home time for this little chicky nuggy."

Gideon groaned as he got to his feet. "And the little chicky nuggy's dadda."

Chapter Seven

GIDEON STAYED TRUE TO HIS WORD ON MAKING DINNER, though it was easy because, at some point in the day, Toby had fully stocked the fridge and pantry.

Was there anything in Gideon's life that Toby didn't manage to perfection?

While Gideon made a cheesy pasta with cherry tomatoes and spinach, Toby bathed Benson and dressed him in his pyjamas. He carried him into the kitchen, blowing a raspberry on his cheek, making him laugh.

It made Gideon pause, his heart thumping a painful beat.

Was it hearing Benson's laughter? Or was it seeing Toby with him? Holding him with such affection, making him laugh like that?

Everything that his asshole ex was not.

Gideon shook his head, snapping any errant thoughts from his mind. Benson's happy face made him smile. And Toby's . . .

Stop it, Gideon. Don't think of him like that.

"Did you go shopping this morning?" Gideon asked, trying to regain his composure.

"Sure did."

Gideon wasn't sure how Toby did it all so effortlessly. When Gideon was on his own with Benson, he could barely get himself showered in a day. Toby did the shopping, appointments, laundry, and trips to the park.

"Here," Toby said, handing Benson over. "I'll serve up dinner. Someone wants Dadda cuddles."

Gideon took Benson, inhaling his clean baby smell. Benson put his hands to Gideon's face, taking a good grip on his moustache. "Ah. No, Benson. Poor, Dadda," he said, trying to pull free.

Toby put two plates on the table. "He loves the 'stache."

Gideon put Benson in his bouncer and brought him over to the table so he could see them while they ate.

"Mm," Toby hummed after his first bite. "This is really good."

He pretended that compliment didn't bolster him more than it did. "Thanks."

They ate in silence for a few bites. "So," Toby said, sipping his water. "The moustache. Have you always had it?"

Gideon smiled as he swallowed his mouthful. "I was at uni, and all the guys were doing Movember," he replied. "You know how they grow a mo and raise money for men's health. Anyway, it was a joke to begin with, but after a month, I was used to it. It suited me, and I liked it. I've had it ever since."

"It does suit you," Toby agreed. "Very Tom Selleck."

That made Gideon snort. "I've heard every Magnum PI joke you can imagine."

Toby chuckled. "Oh, I can imagine." He ate a few more

bites. "So, I wanted to run something past you, and it's completely your call."

Gideon wasn't sure he liked the sound of this . . .

"When I was at the supermarket today, I bought some Farex."

Gideon almost choked on his pasta. He had to cough and sip his water before he could speak. "Some *what*?"

Toby stared at him plainly. "Farex. It's a rice cereal for babies. Why, what did you think it was?"

His face was burning. "I thought you said something else."

Toby laughed at first, then his eyes cut to Gideon's. "Oh my god, did you think I said Lurex?" Obviously surprised and laughing, he shook his head. "Uh, no. Because that's not what I said. It explains your reaction though."

Yes, because buying condoms or lube would be appropriate dinner conversation, Gideon. Jeez.

Toby was clearly amused, not even a little embarrassed. "No, I said Farex. It's usually a lead up to their first solid food. Anyway, given Benson here is having bigger bottles more frequently now, I wondered if you'd like to try him on some Farex. It's completely up to you, of course. Only when you think he's ready. I thought I'd grab some when I saw it today, just in case. That's all."

Gideon looked at Toby, then to Benson. He was in his bouncer, but he was kicking a bit now and starting to get cranky.

"Do you think he's ready?" Gideon asked. Sure, he'd noticed Benson was drinking bigger bottles, and more often, and he'd attributed the grizzles to teething. "Oh my god, have I been starving him?"

Toby reached across and squeezed Gideon's hand. "No. Absolutely not—"

67

"Because I don't know these things. But I should, shouldn't I." That was not a question, because Gideon *should* know these things. Of course he should know these things. "Oh god—"

"Okay, stop!" Toby's hold on Gideon's hand tightened, and it worked because Gideon stopped. "You're not starving him. He's perfectly healthy and happy. And you're not expected to know everything."

"But you know everything."

He scoffed. "No I don't. I've just looked after babies before. How many babies have you looked after?"

"Well . . . none."

"And I have a degree in child development," Toby added. "It's my job to know."

And I'm his father. It's my job to know too.

Toby shook his head, smiling almost. "Nah-uh. I know what you're thinking. That you're his dad and you should have known. We're not doing the whole guilt thing."

"How did you know that's what I was thinking?"

He chuckled and patted Gideon's hand before sitting back in his seat. "Because I know that's exactly where your mind would have gone because you're a good father, Gideon."

The back of Gideon's hand still felt the heat of Toby's touch, but he tried his best to ignore it. Instead, he turned his attention to Benson. "Do you think he's ready?"

It was a redundant question, Gideon realised, because Toby wouldn't have bought the damn stuff if he didn't think Benson was ready for it.

Toby gave him a soft smile. "We can only try. If he's not ready, he'll let us know. But you should be the one to feed him. First solid food—it's a date to write in his baby book."

Gideon found himself smiling. He didn't know how

Toby did it. He eased his fears and reassured him and reminded him that he was doing okay. Toby was an endless well of support, knowing exactly what to say and when to say it. It was the kind of support he'd hoped to get from Drew; instead, he got the opposite.

Toby was a whole bunch of things that Drew never was.

Sure, Gideon was paying for Toby's kind words and kind heart, but he wasn't sure if he cared about the technicality. Toby made Gideon happy, and even if it was a professional obligation, Gideon would take it.

"Look who it is," Toby said. He was bouncing Benson on his knee, both of them smiling as Gideon came out in his pyjamas. "Dadda, look at who's a big boy and slept right through the night."

Gideon stopped, his smile widening. "He did?"

Toby stood and carried Benson like he was an aeroplane, complete with the vroom sound effects, straight into Gideon's arms. "He sure did."

"I didn't hear him," Gideon confessed. "I just assumed you got up. I think I'm still recovering from drinking alcohol and sleeping on the floor. I'm sorry." He gave Toby an apologetic smile, then blew a raspberry on Benson's cheek. "A big boy, huh? He slept right through?"

Toby nodded. "Woke up just before six. He's had a bottle this morning, but we might try some more Farex."

"Do you think that's why he slept through? Having a full belly?" Gideon asked.

"Probably." Toby shrugged, even though he did think it was likely. "How about I make us a coffee?"

Toby left them and set about making two mugs of

coffee, he could hear Gideon murmuring and Benson's answering giggles. It was the sweetest sound.

Gideon followed him into the kitchen and leaned against the counter, holding Benson close and pretending to take gummy bites out of his belly, making him laugh.

Toby put Gideon's coffee on the counter next to him. "Someone's being extra cute today."

Gideon smiled at him in a way that Toby wasn't quite prepared for. Gideon was sleep rumpled in his blue pyjama pants and white T-shirt, his hair a mess, and three-day growth, but that smile . . .

It was warm and somehow personal, and it made Toby's stomach swoop.

What the hell?

Christ, Toby. Get a grip.

Gideon was just in a good mood, he was happy, and he was being cute with his son. That look, those eyes were full of affection for Benson.

Toby had to remind himself of that.

He sipped his coffee and turned toward the pantry. "How about I get a second breakfast ready for this little Hobbit," Toby said. "Then you can go get ready for work."

He wasn't really asking. He already had the Farex out.

"Are you sure?" Gideon asked.

"Yeah, sure. But just so you know, when he starts eating actual food, I can't do mushed up banana. Babies love it but it makes me gag, so you'll be doing all of that. I can do just about anything, but not mushy or cooked bananas."

Gideon smiled as he sipped his coffee, Benson now on his hip. "Deal. But does that mean you don't even like banana bread?"

Toby screwed his face up. "Ew, no."

"Not even toasted?"

He almost gagged at the thought. "Especially not hot. That makes it worse."

Gideon chuckled. "How did I not know this?"

"Because we've never had the 'what food makes you vomit' conversation."

"True. Though we have discussed coriander. And kale."

"We have."

"What do you order from a café for brunch if you don't have banana bread? Banana bread and coffee is my staple."

"Literally anything else. French toast reigns supreme." Toby mixed the Farex in a bowl. "Although brunch can go either way. You can order a full breakfast or a piece of cheesecake. A yoghurt bowl with fresh berries, or the fried chicken and waffles. There are no rules at brunch."

There was that warm, personal smile again. "No rules at all."

Avoiding another rush of butterflies, Toby turned back to mixing the rice cereal, runny enough to almost be in Benson's bottle. The pale goop was a good distraction and he let some drip off the spoon. "Is the cutest little Hobbit ready for his second breakfast?"

Toby fed Benson while Gideon showered, and Toby almost had Benson all cleaned up by the time Gideon reappeared in his suit. "I think we wore more than we ate," Toby volunteered. "But he likes it, and he's a happy little munchkin today."

Gideon snorted. "Munchkin's new. So is little Hobbit."

Toby smiled proudly. "He'll always be a little chicky nuggy."

Gideon grinned, disappearing into the kitchen, and a few moments later, he came out holding a plate with a piece of peanut butter toast. He handed it to Toby. "For you."

"Oh." Toby was surprised by the gesture, as simple as it was. "Thank you."

Gideon bit into his own piece. "Not sure what time I'll be home," he said. "After I was out most of yesterday, I'll probably have to catch up."

"No problem," Toby replied. "We still right to Face-Time you at one o'clock?"

Gideon collected his car keys and gave Toby a huge smile. "Absolutely."

TOBY HANDED GIDEON A CUP OF TEA WITH A SQUARE OF dark chocolate before he sat down on the couch, just as Toby's favourite baking show came on. Gideon had just put a sound-asleep Benson to bed in his crib, and he looked tired.

"Long day?" Toby asked. They hadn't really had a chance to speak since he got home.

Gideon sipped his tea and hummed. "It was. Work, a phone call with my lawyer." He glanced at Toby. "And more work."

"Oh, is everything okay?" Toby asked. "With your lawyer."

"Yeah. She just wanted to clarify a few things that the associate and I discussed yesterday. It was all fine. Just . . . draining." Then he smiled. "Nice to come home though. Getting to do bath-time and dinner with Benson is my highlight. Dinner was great too, thank you."

"You're welcome."

"One hundred percent know I couldn't do this without you."

Toby's chest burned, right in behind his sternum. "I'm sure you could."

Not that Toby wanted to think about Gideon doing any of this without him.

Gideon snorted, even rolled his eyes a little. "Exceedingly unlikely."

Toby ignored the cute smile and turned his attention back to the baking show on TV. "Oh my god, they're making banana bread. You jinxed me."

Gideon's laughter was deep and warm, and Toby did his best to ignore how happy that sound made him.

The next night they watched back-to-back episodes of *Drag Race*, and the night after that, they binged some episodes of those ridiculously expensive mansions on tropical islands. They had cups of raspberry tea and small squares of dark chocolate, and they laughed and talked, and Toby knew this wasn't like his other jobs.

He'd always just spent evenings and nights in his room. He'd always maintained that professional distance.

He'd never wanted to spend time with any of his other employers.

But Gideon wasn't like them.

He was a single dad, for a start. He'd been through a terrible break up and he appreciated Toby's company.

And he was gay. Everyone else Toby had worked for was very heterosexual, which had never been an issue, of course. But there was a solidarity in working for a fellow queer man. Especially one who was doing everything humanly possible to be the best parent he could be.

Toby respected him.

He sympathised with him. He understood him.

He liked him.

"What are your plans for this weekend?" Gideon asked.

Toby hadn't realised the TV show had finished. He drained the rest of the tea from his cup. "Any crazy family dinners?"

Toby shook his head with a smile. "No. My brother's been pestering me to hit the clubs with him. I think I'm out of excuses."

Gideon looked as if he had eaten something bad but didn't want to offend the cook. Then he tried to smile, but that didn't quite sit right either. "You should go, have some fun."

"It's Josh's idea of fun. Not really mine. I'm much more of a stay-in kinda guy."

Gideon's eyes met Toby's and his smile was much more natural. "Same. Well, I am now. I'm too old for that shit."

"You're not old."

"My body disagrees. I got hammered last Sunday night and I'm still not over it."

Toby chuckled. "It wasn't the Scotch that did the damage. It was sleeping on the tiny sofa and the floor."

"It was all of it. Believe me."

"Probably." Toby found himself smiling at him. "But tell me this. If you didn't have Benson, if you were single, had no responsibilities, and could do whatever you wanted, what would you be doing this weekend?"

He took a second to consider it, then sighed. "I'd be sitting on my couch in my comfy trackies, drinking raspberry tea and watching TV shows about ridiculous mansions on some private island in Thailand."

Toby laughed. "You would not."

"I absolutely would." Gideon stuck out his foot to show off his track pants and tapped his teacup. "Living the dream right here."

Toby smiled at him because damn, if that wasn't Toby's dream too.

Not that he said that out loud.

The next night, right on six o'clock, Josh arrived to pick Toby up. He had exactly forty-eight hours to rest, relax, and get his head right, and it couldn't have come a moment too soon.

Gideon had been home for half an hour and was feeding Benson. Just sitting on the couch in his work suit, giving Benson a bottle, both of them smiling at each other.

Toby had to make himself leave.

He threw his bag in the backseat of Josh's car and climbed into the front. "Hey," Josh said, his usual grin in place. "Dinner with the parentals, because Mum said we had to, and then we are going out. You're not getting out of it . . ." His words trailed off as he studied Toby. "What's wrong?"

Toby shot his brother a quick look, his stomach in a giant knot. "I think I'm in trouble."

Josh stopped smiling. "What do you mean? Did something happen?"

"No, nothing bad. The opposite probably. I don't know. Jesus."

"Oh my god. You like him!"

"Shut up," Toby hissed. "And can you drive? We're parked out the front of his house like freaking weirdos."

He started the engine, his smile now a shit-eating grin. "You got a thing for the Tom Selleck moustache."

"It's not a thing. It's just . . . I keep thinking . . . over-thinking, more like it." Toby let out a sharp breath and put his hands out like a that's-final gesture. "He's my boss and I live in his house, and this is absurd and can only end in tears. My tears, that is. Just because he's insanely gorgeous and incredibly sweet and funny and—"

"Holy shit. You actually like this guy."

75

"Can you drive, please?"

Josh pulled out onto the street and was quiet for a block or two. Toby wasn't too sure; his mind was spinning in circles.

He wasn't about to tell Josh about the almost-kiss that had nearly happened last Sunday night. He wasn't about to tell him about how he'd wanted Gideon to kiss him. He wasn't going to tell him how they talked every night over stupid cups of tea, or how they FaceTime every day at lunchtime. Well, the FaceTiming was for Benson, but seeing Gideon smile when he saw Benson, seeing and hearing the way he'd talk to him, was a highlight of Toby's day.

He couldn't explain any of this to Josh. Because Josh would be a voice of reason and say things like 'you need to stop' or 'maybe you should find another family to nanny for' and Toby just didn't want to hear that.

"Tobes," Josh said. "You know what I think?"

Toby sighed. "I don't want to hear—"

"You need to go out tonight, get drunk as fuck, and hook up with some rando."

Oh.

Toby stared at him then snorted out a laugh. It was not what he'd expected him to say at all. But maybe that *was* what he needed. It had been a while since he'd hooked up with anyone. Some drunken hand job in a London night-club bathroom to be exact . . .

God, it had been a while.

"You know what?" Toby said. "I think you might be right."

Chapter Eight

"I think I'm in trouble," Gideon said. He stabbed his pork dumpling and frowned at Lauren and Jill. They were out for Sunday lunch at Lauren's favourite Japanese restaurant, Benson asleep in his pram.

He hadn't had his morning sleep on Saturday or Sunday because Gideon wasn't Toby and apparently Toby was the only one who could get Benson to have a morning nap.

"Trouble with what?" Lauren asked. "I thought you said your solicitor—"

"No, no. All the legal stuff is fine. Well, it's not *fine*. But my solicitor's on top of it."

She reached out and covered Gideon's hand with her own. "Then who are you in trouble with?"

Jill answered. "Toby."

Gideon sighed and pushed his fork away, giving up any hope of eating. His stomach was one big rolling mess. "Yes, Toby."

Lauren made a sad face. "Oh dear."

"I shouldn't be thinking of him like that. I shouldn't be

thinking of anyone like that. I am not looking for anything. I am sworn off all men forever." Gideon sighed. "But he's . . ."

Lauren tilted her head. "He's . . . ?"

"He's everything I wanted Drew to be. He's everything I need. And I'm paying him to be everything I need, so it's even more fucked up than it sounds. God." He put his hand to his forehead. "We laugh every night watching stupid shows on TV, and he's thoughtful and kind, and funny, and he's so good with Benson. Benson's face when he sees him, he just lights up." He put his hand to his heart. "I'm in so much trouble."

Lauren was quiet for a long moment, though Gideon didn't miss the exchange of looks between Jill and Lauren. "Okay," Lauren began. "So, let's look at this objectively. He's come into your life when everything was shit. You were exhausted and miserable. And his help has been a saving grace, right?"

Gideon nodded. "Yes."

"He's made your life easier, considerably so."

"Yes," Gideon said. "One hundred percent."

"So is it possible that you could be seeing him in that light? You said he's everything you wanted Drew to be. Which is what, exactly?"

"Caring. Attentive. Kind."

"With Benson."

"Yes. He's so good with him. But not just with Benson, with me as well. We talk and laugh, more than I ever did with Drew. And we make each other coffee and toast in the mornings. Some mornings," he amended. "Not every morning. God, this isn't good."

Lauren patted his hand. "Do you think it's possible that you're seeing more than what's there? Drew treated you like absolute shit and broke your heart, and then along comes a guy who treats you nicely. And all I'm saying is that when you've been treated poorly, it's easy to mistake kindness for affection."

Gideon could see her point, and he knew there were good intentions to her honesty. He conceded a nod, then sighed with his head in his hands. "His brother was taking him out to some nightclub this weekend, and all I keep thinking about is him hooking up with some other guy."

"Oh no," Jill mumbled.

He looked up at her. "I know! I mean, he *should be* going out with his brother and having a great time, hooking up with whoever he wants. He's young, single, and incredibly good looking. But fuck, the thought of him with someone else . . . I barely slept, and I stuffed up Benson's sleep schedule after Toby worked hard all week to get him into a routine."

"Hmm," Jill hummed. "Yeah, when I said, 'oh no,' it wasn't like 'oh no, that's terrible,' it was more of a 'oh no, you really do have it bad for him' kind of 'oh no'."

Gideon let his head fall back with a groan. "I tried not to, because it has disaster written all over it. I tried to ignore it, but since we almost kissed in my kitchen—"

"You what?" they said in unison.

Gideon sighed. "He hugged me when I was—"

Lauren's eyes were wide. "He hugged you?"

"Hm, okay, Gideon, I love you dearly," Jill said, "so I'm just going to ask you outright. No judgement at all. Do you want us to talk you out of it, or do you want to pursue this?"

He stared at her. "I don't know. Both. Neither." He shook his head. "No, please talk me out of it. Tell me this is stupidly inappropriate, and I'd be a fool to take my actual saving grace and ruin it. I'm his boss, technically. He lives with me, and I need him to stay in my life. I can't take on a full mortgage and be Benson's full-time carer. I need to provide for him and having Toby in my life allows me to do that."

Lauren gave him a sad smile. "That's a lot of good points."

"Your point was good too! The one about mistaking his kindness for affection." Gideon nodded quickly. "That totally tracks. Because I don't think I know what it even means to be treated nicely by a man. I don't know. I'm so screwed."

"I'm just trying to be a voice of reason," Lauren added. "I want you to be happy, but I know your happiness will come from keeping your house and providing a good life for Benson."

Gideon nodded.

"I want you to have both," Jill countered.

"Jilly," Lauren said, her tone matching the warning in her eyes. "Not helping."

Jill just smiled and shrugged it off. "Why can't he have both? Why can't he have a relationship with Toby? If it's consensual and they're happy, then why not?"

"Because it gets complicated," Lauren said. "If they fight or break up, then he'll need to find a new nanny, and he doesn't want that. He wants Toby."

Jill's frown said she didn't exactly agree with that. "Complicated, yes. And being sensible is probably the right thing to do. But Gideon, what if taking that risk turns into the best thing to ever happen to you?"

Gideon looked at them both and sighed. "I feel like I have a little angel and a little devil on each shoulder, each trying to sway my decision."

Jill laughed quietly. "I just want you to be happy."

"So do I, Gideon," Lauren added. "I just don't want to see you dive headfirst into something without checking the water first, yeah?"

Gideon met her gaze. "You always were the sensible one."

Jill laughed at that. "That's not true. But here's my last piece of advice. You said he was going out this weekend? So maybe he hooked up with a few guys and—"

"Oh god," Gideon said, making a face. The thought of Toby with anyone else made his stomach feel all greasy.

Jill put her hand on Gideon's arm. "If he did, then that's your answer. Save yourself all the stress and conflict because he's not on the same page."

"But," Lauren added, "just because he didn't hook up with someone doesn't mean he wants to settle down with you."

Gideon winced. "I think I like Jill better today."

Lauren laughed. "Sounds like you need to either talk to him about the page you're on. Or forget about the whole thing."

He knew what she was saying made perfect sense. He just wished it wasn't all so hard. "I'm not ready for anything serious anyway," he admitted. "I just need to forget about the whole thing. Concentrate on me for a while. Me and Benson, no one else."

Lauren nodded, and Jill did too. Sort of. "Unless he's gorgeous and sweet, and also happens to be the nanny who adoooooores your son."

Both Lauren and Gideon groaned, and Jill shrugged. "What?" she said, looking at Gideon. "I saw how he looked at you when you were shit-faced drunk. He was concerned and worried for you."

Lauren conceded a nod with a sigh. "That's true."

Jill wasn't done. "I'm telling you, he's probably with his brother right now having the same conversation about you that we're having about him."

Gideon shook his head. He didn't really believe that at all. "As nice as the idea is, and that is a really nice thought, let's be real. I'm not in any place to be thinking about anyone else just yet. I'm certainly not in any position emotionally to be thinking of another relationship."

Gideon spoke with enough conviction to almost convince himself.

Almost.

———

Toby smiled as he walked up to the house just before six, with grilled fish, chips, and salad from the place he knew Gideon liked. It wasn't too far out of his way, even though Josh had ribbed him about going the extra mile for his boss. Toby had ignored him, like he'd ignored everything his stupid brother had said all weekend about Toby liking Gideon.

It had been a long weekend and Toby was looking forward to going back to work. He'd missed Benson, and he'd missed Gideon, though he wasn't admitting that to anyone.

Least of all Josh.

He came through the door, and Gideon was on the couch with a spoon while Benson was in the rocker. "Hey," Gideon said, smiling at him.

Toby couldn't help it. He felt instantly at ease, like he was coming home to his own house: a warm, fuzzy feeling he hadn't felt at any other job he'd worked at. "Hey," he said. He dumped his overnight bag and held up the takeout. "I got your favourite fish and salad."

Gideon picked Benson up and sat him on his knee. "Look who it is," he said.

Toby put the takeout on the dining table and picked up Benson. He was covered in Farex as if he'd worn more than he'd eaten, and he gave Toby a huge gummy smile.

"Look at how cute you are!" Toby said, wiping off the Farex with Benson's bib. Once his face was somewhat clean, he gave him a few fish-bubble kisses on his chubby cheek.

Benson laughed and the sound settled in Toby's chest.

"I ruined his sleep schedule," Gideon said, taking the plate and spoon to the sink. "I don't know how, exactly, because you were only gone for two days, and it all went to shit. He didn't want morning sleeps but then slept more at lunchtime, then he had a quick nap this afternoon, like a battery recharge, and he wanted dinner now."

Toby chuckled and gave Gideon's arm a reassuring pat. "You didn't ruin anything. Someone here," he said, giving Benson's button nose a gentle boop, "probably thinks he's a big boy chicky nugget now, who doesn't need morning sleeps anymore. That's all."

Gideon took a warm washcloth and wiped Benson's face properly. "Thanks," he said, giving Toby a small smile.

And that right there was why Toby spent the weekend all bent out of shape.

The smile, the kind eyes, the warm rumble of laughter . . .

"Thanks for bringing dinner," Gideon said. "And for getting it from my favourite place."

"It's my favourite fish place too," Toby said. Admittedly,

it was his only fish and chips place, given he'd only had fish from one place since he'd been back, but that was beside the point.

If it made Gideon look at him like that, he'd admit to nothing.

So while Benson was happy to lay under his play gym, Toby and Gideon ate their dinner. "How was the rest of your weekend?" Toby asked. "Besides someone deciding he didn't need morning sleeps anymore."

"It was good," Gideon said. "I got nothing done. I don't know how you do it all. Okay, so I managed a few loads of laundry, and I did leave the house today for lunch with Lauren and Jill. But that's it. That's all I did."

"Sounds like a great weekend to me," Toby said. He wasn't lying or being sarcastic.

"How was yours?" Gideon asked. He stabbed at his salad as if trying to be nonchalant, but it only made him look more . . . curious? Nervous? "You said Josh wanted you to go out clubbing with him?"

"Ugh." Toby made a face. "Friday night. It was okay. Loud, obnoxious. I only had a few drinks but, god, clubbing really isn't my scene. Maybe when I was eighteen, but now I'd much rather—" He gestured between them. "Well, this."

Then, much too late, he realised how that sounded.

"I didn't mean this as in us." He did the stupid waving between them thing again. "Not that that'd be—not that I think you and I—" *Shut up, Toby. Just shut up and stop talking.* His face was burning so hot he almost started to sweat. "What I meant was—"

Gideon surprised him by laughing. "I know what you mean. I prefer this too." He waved his fork between them, then to Benson, then around the room. "I'd take *this* over clubbing any day." His eyes met Toby's and he held his gaze. Something flickered in the blue grey. *Was that a look? What the hell was that?* Toby's mind was reeling when Gideon shrugged it away. "Even when I was eighteen and at uni, I always preferred having a few drinks in the dorms rather than pubs or clubs."

"Less hassle, less money."

"And less idiots."

"Oh god, isn't that the truth. Josh being one of them. I spent all night babysitting him and making sure he got home in one piece. And that he didn't shag anyone in the bathrooms."

"I thought he was taking you out to get you drunk?"

"He was. It was a mission failure. Actually, the whole night was a bust, to be honest."

He wasn't admitting to Gideon that he'd spent most of the night wondering how Gideon and Benson were getting on . . .

Gideon's smile was hard to read. If Toby wasn't mistaken, Gideon seemed pleased that Toby's night had been a bust. That he hadn't got drunk and shagged anyone in the bathrooms . . .

Surely not.

Surely Toby was misreading that.

"Then he was hungover as a dog on Saturday, and in a filthy mood," Toby added. "So Dad made him mow the lawn."

Gideon laughed. "That's brutal."

"But not undeserved."

"I thought you were going to say you had a two-day bender and had to rifle through some random guy's mail before he woke up to get an address for the taxi home."

Toby snorted. "That's oddly specific. Speaking from experience?"

Gideon chuckled. "A long time ago."

Toby ate the last of his dinner. "No. There was no two-day bender, no going through some hook-up's mail to find an address. Though I'm sure we have maps now, and Uber. But no, no hook-ups at all. Have you seen what's out there lately?" He shook his head. "Yeah, that's all a big no from me."

"I haven't looked in a long, long time. Clearly before we had maps on our phones, or Uber."

Toby knew this was heading into personal territory, but he wanted to know, and he wasn't the one who brought up the random hook-up detail. "Do you think you'll ever brave the dating scene again?"

Gideon's gaze shot to his, and he shook his head. "Uh, no. I don't imagine so."

Toby decided to lighten the conversation. "Well, if you decide to go the old-fashioned way of meeting in a bar instead of Grindr, just so you now, the guys at the clubs on George Street are not it."

Gideon smiled with a sigh and pushed his plate away. "I think that part of my life is over for a while," he said. "I was just talking to Lauren and Jill about this today, actually. It'll be good to focus on me and Benson for a while." He chewed on his bottom lip for a second. "What about you? Will you brave the dating scene now you're back in Sydney?"

Toby shook his head. "Nah. I'm too busy. Plus, I have you and Benson." Toby froze. "Oh, I didn't mean for that to sound like that. I just meant that I'm busy, and I don't miss hanging out with anyone because I hang out with you guys during the week, Benson during the day, you at night, then on weekends I see my family. I didn't mean that we . . ."

God, his stupid mouth would never save him from embarrassing himself.

Gideon chuckled and waved him off. "I said something similar to Lauren and Jill. We watch TV and have a laugh most nights, and that's more than I ever did with Drew." Then he winced. "Not that what we do is like that . . ."

Gideon finished with a shrug and they both had pink cheeks. Before either of them could embarrass themselves even more, Benson decided he'd had enough playing.

Toby stood up. "I'll clean up while you get him ready for bed."

Gideon stood as well. "Thank you," he said quietly. "For dinner."

He looked as if he wanted to say something else, but collected Benson and took him into the bathroom, and Toby took a second to collect himself. He stood at the kitchen sink, catching his breath.

His and Gideon's conversation had well and truly delved into personal territory, and they'd both kind of admitted that they enjoyed hanging out with each other. That neither of them was looking for anything with anyone else because what they had was enough.

Gideon wasn't looking for anything right now, which Toby understood. And Toby wasn't looking because . . . because he wanted what he had with Gideon.

Did he want more?

Yes.

Would he risk his job for it?

No.

He needed common sense to prevail.

So he cleaned up dinner, then went and made his bed. He'd washed his sheets before he'd left but hadn't had time to remake it before Josh picked hm up on Friday night. And when he was finished, he found himself in the hallway, listening to Gideon sing to Benson as he gave him his bath.

And Toby's heart thumped a little harder.

And later that night, when Gideon was putting Benson to bed, Toby tried not to listen even though he knew what he would hear.

"Dadda loves you," he murmured. "To the moon and back."

Toby's heart thumped again, and he knew that maybe it was too late for common sense.

All the reasoning and rationale in the world wasn't going to help him. He definitely had feelings for Gideon. Did he want to spend nights curled on the same couch instead of sitting separately? Yes. Did he want to know what it felt like to kiss him with that moustache?

Toby had thought about that a lot.

Not that it changed anything. He certainly wasn't going to act on it.

That *would* be crossing the line.

"Would you like a cup of tea?" Gideon asked.

Toby hadn't heard him come out of Benson's room. "Oh, sure," he replied quickly, his hand to his heart. "Sorry, I was a million miles away."

Thinking about kissing you.

He watched Toby for a long moment. "Raspberry tea?"

"Yes, please."

TOBY TRIED TO IGNORE THE FEELING IN HIS BELLY every time he saw Gideon. But every night they would watch TV together, with a cup of tea and a lot of laughs. He'd go to bed happy, confused, and a little heartsore.

Every night that week.

And every day at lunchtime when Toby would Face-Time Gideon at work, his smiling face on the screen made Toby's stomach swoop with butterflies, and it made his heart stutter.

Sure, Gideon mostly smiled for Benson, but when Toby would hold Benson and say, "Say bye-bye to Dadda. Can't wait to see you when you get home," and he'd wave Benson's little hand, Gideon's eyes would soften and he'd smile at Toby in a way that made his heart ache.

"Thank you," he'd say quietly, as if Toby had just given him the greatest gift instead of a two-minute video chat.

Every day.

And every day that burning ember behind his ribs got a little bit harder to ignore.

On Thursday, Benson had been disgruntled most of the day. He was teething, his two bottom teeth were almost through, and he spent all of his FaceTime with Gideon chewing on his fist and crying.

"Need me to come home?" Gideon asked.

"No, it's fine," Toby replied. "He's also tired. I'm sure he'll feel better if he goes down for a nap."

Gideon nodded. "Want me to bring home dinner?"

Toby shook his head. "No, it's fine. I just put some chicken in the slow cooker. Just a sticky chicken recipe I saw on TikTok. I'll make some rice when you get home."

"I don't know what sticky chicken is, but I'll take your word for it. It sounds good, anyway." Gideon gave him one of those special smiles—one of those just-for-you smiles—and Toby's heart stuttered.

Toby had to make himself look away before he said something stupid. It was time to go anyway, so he gave Benson's hand a little wave. "Say bye-bye, Dadda."

Gideon leaned in close to the screen and waved back. "Benson, you be a good boy for Toby." Then his gaze cut to Toby's and he held it. "Call me if you need anything."

"Okay."

When Gideon got home, he'd no sooner put his keys and wallet down before Toby was flying Benson airplane-style into his arms. "Someone needs Dadda cuddles."

He took him and gave Benson a kiss on the cheek. "Still fussing?"

Toby rubbed Benson's back. "A little. He's really not too bad. No temp, just teething. Has teething poops, which are gross. Poor little guy. He's had some dinner, but he might want an early bath, bottle, and bed, I think."

Gideon smiled as he headed toward the bathroom. "Dinner smells good."

Toby checked the chicken. It didn't look like the videos he'd seen on TikTok, but he had used chicken from the freezer. He'd double-checked it was cooked—he always double-checked chicken—because he'd been late getting it into the slow cooker. When he dished it up, he served it with an apology. "It doesn't look very sticky," he said. It had way more liquid than the pictures . . .

"I'm sure it'll be fine," Gideon replied.

And it tasted fine. It wasn't the best thing he'd ever made, but it was easy enough. And when they were done, Toby cleaned up while Gideon gave Benson a bottle and put him to bed.

When he came out, he went straight to the couch. They watched some TV, and after a while, he noticed Gideon shifting in his seat a bit. He pushed against his stomach, making a face.

Toby didn't want to admit that he felt much the same. "Would you like a cup of tea?"

Gideon shook his head. "No, I don't think I will tonight, but thanks."

Thank god.

It was the last thing Toby wanted.

"Might go and have a shower," Gideon said.

Toby nodded, and the longer he sat there, the worse he felt. He changed into his PJs and he wondered if some soda water might help.

Then the hot and cold sweats started, and the stomach cramps.

He went in search of Gideon and found him sitting on the edge of his bed. He looked uncomfortable and pale.

"You okay?" Toby asked.

Gideon shook his head.

"Me either."

Gideon let out a shaky breath, then dashed for his en suite bathroom. As soon as Toby heard him vomit, his own stomach roiled and heaved, and he had to run to the bathroom as well.

He barely made it in time.

He sat on the edge of the bathtub, feeling steadily worse. Hot and cold, sweating and shivering, and terrible stomach cramps. He vomited again and again, wanting to lie down on the cold tiles but refraining.

He managed to find some washcloths. He wet them both and knocked on Gideon's door. He answered with only a groan and a flushing toilet. He was leaning against his bathroom vanity, a ghastly shade of green.

When he looked in the en suite mirror, Toby realised he looked much the same.

He handed Gideon the washcloth. "Think it was bad chicken," he said.

As soon as Toby mentioned it, Gideon vomited again, and Toby had to run back to his bathroom.

An eternity of hell later, when the diarrhoea started, Toby did what any self-respecting grown man would do. He found his phone and called for help.

"Mum?"

Chapter Nine

FOOD POISONING.

Brutal, indescribable, indiscriminate.

Unforgiving.

Gideon couldn't remember ever being so ill.

In his fitful sleep, he thought he saw Toby sitting on the floor by Gideon's bed, leaning against the wall, a bucket by his side.

He would have thought it was sweet if he weren't so ill.

If he couldn't be sure he'd not imagined it.

Gideon wasn't sure if he'd imagined the sound of voices either. A woman's voice, soft and distant.

The stomach cramps and cold sweats, and exhaustion, made it impossible to focus. Or care.

He felt like death had pummelled him, keeping him a few inches from dying just for laughs.

Then, when a woman appeared beside his bed and wiped his face with a cool cloth, he was sure she was an angel . . . "Did I die?" he asked.

The woman laughed quietly, dabbing his forehead. "No, sweetheart."

"Benson?"

"Sound asleep in his crib."

Gideon slept then, relieved and reassured.

Until he had to run for the bathroom again.

He considered sleeping on the toilet but managed to drag himself back to bed . . . to find a lump on the other side of the bed.

No, not a lump.

A person.

Toby.

In his bed?

Surely he was dreaming.

He knew Toby was ill too. He'd heard him be sick at the beginning of this nightmare.

But Gideon was too sick, too sore, too tired to care.

He simply climbed back into bed and closed his eyes.

He knew if Toby felt as ill as Gideon did, there was no way he could look after Benson in the morning. Gideon would have to get up. As Benson's father, it was his job to care for him, whether Gideon was sick or not. He could only hope the pains, the vomiting, and diarrhoea, would be gone by the time Benson woke up.

Just a few more hours.

Surely he'd feel better in a few hours . . .

HE WOKE WITH A START AND SAW IT WAS LIGHT BEHIND the blinds in his room. He grabbed his phone to check the time.

8:34 am.

Gideon shot out of bed, only noticing that Toby was asleep beside him—he hadn't imagined that—and he dashed for the door . . . only for his stomach to protest violently.

He got to the hall, gripping his stomach with one hand, the wall with his other. He noticed Benson's door was open, the TV was on, and Benson's happy babbling was coming from the lounge room.

What the hell?

Gideon walked out to find a woman sitting on his couch. Benson was in his rocker, smiling away with his fist in his mouth.

"Oh dear," the woman said. She was fifty-ish, had a brown bob and a kind face. "You should be back in bed. You look dreadful."

He pushed against his stomach. He was sure he couldn't vomit anything else up, but the cramps were pitiful. "Uh, thanks?"

"I'm Carla, Toby's mum. He called me late last night to come and look after your little one for you."

Gideon's head swam.

"Just as well he did," Carla said. "Neither of you are in any shape to. And this little jelly bean is the cutest baby I think I've ever seen. Sweet as sugar." She stood up and ushered Gideon back to his room. "So you rest and take it easy. Back to bed. Everything is taken care of."

Gideon felt like he was in an episode of *The Twilight Zone.*

"I put Toby in your bed because he got a little vomit in his, and I had to remake it. Plus, this bathroom was closer," she said, helping Gideon lie down. "And I'll be sleeping in his room until you're better."

He groaned as soon as his head hit the pillow. He wasn't sure what to say. He wasn't sure on any of what she'd just said.

He still wasn't sure if he was dreaming . . .

When he opened his eyes next, Carla was putting a glass beside his bed. "Some Lucozade. Sip it when you're able." She felt his forehead. "Your temperature's going down. Just gotta ride it out, I'm afraid."

She felt his forehead?

She brought him a drink?

She was taking care of Benson?

Did she call Benson a jelly bean earlier?

Toby groaned beside him. "Mum?"

"Oh, sweetheart," she said, going to his side of the bed. "I'll get you some Lucozade too. You feeling better?"

"Benson," he murmured with another groan.

"He's fine," she said, feeling his forehead now. "Back to sleep, both of you."

It had been so long since Gideon had had any kind of mother-figure fuss over him. He wasn't sure what to make of it, but he was thankful she was here. He was so exhausted, and sore all over, he did exactly what she'd told him to do and closed his eyes.

———

HE WOKE UP WHEN TOBY SNUGGLED INTO HIS BACK, groaning in discomfort as he settled. He was warm against Gideon's back. The body of another man was something Gideon hadn't felt in a long time. He never realised how much he'd missed the contact. Was he *that* touch-starved?

Maybe it was just comforting because he was sick. God, it felt good.

GIDEON WOKE UP, FACING THE OTHER WALL, WITH HIS arm slung over Toby's ribs. Toby was on his back, sound asleep, thank god. Gideon was tempted to not move his arm. He didn't want to. He wanted this comfort for as long as he could have it.

But then Toby rolled over and faced him, and Gideon's arm fell between them. Toby's eyes flickered open, barely, and Gideon dared not even breathe. Toby almost smiled before he was back asleep. He didn't look so green now, but still pale.

Still beautiful.

Even more so when he slept.

Gideon's stomach twisted and rolled, a sharp reminder that the food poisoning was still in charge. He closed his eyes.

GIDEON GROANED AS HE ROLLED OUT OF BED, WITH barely enough strength to get to the bathroom. Afterwards, he scrubbed his hands like a surgeon, then his face, and then barely made it back to bed. He sipped the Lucozade and fell back into bed with a groan.

"Not good," Toby mumbled.

"Mm-hmm," Gideon agreed.

THE NEXT TIME HE WOKE, HE MADE HIMSELF GET UP TO go check on Benson. Carla had him perched up watching a movie together, having a great time apparently.

"I'm really sorry," Gideon said. "I'm so grateful you're here. Is he okay? Does he need anything?"

"He's fine. We've had the best day," she said. Then she frowned. "You should go back to bed, hun."

Gideon could feel himself fading and he'd only walked a few metres and stood for a few seconds. "Yeah," he said with a nod. He was dying to hold Benson, to hold him and cuddle him, but he didn't want to go near him while he was ill.

"He's fine," she said, softer this time. "But you need rest."

Gideon's whole body was heavy and sore, and he shuffled back to bed. He sipped his drink again and slumped onto his pillow, too tired to even groan.

HE WAS WOKEN UP BY TOBY SHOVING HIM AWAY AND racing for the bathroom. Gideon must have been draped over him again without even realising. When Toby crawled back to bed, he looked miserable.

"You okay?" Gideon asked.

Toby's eyes were closed, a deep frown in place. "My asshole hasn't been this sore since that sex party in Paris."

Gideon stared at him, and Toby's eyes flew open like he'd just realised what he'd said—and to whom.

Gideon burst out laughing, not sure what was funnier: what Toby'd said or the look on his face. But Gideon had to hold his stomach, and his back ached dreadfully. His laughter was soon a groan.

Toby rolled over, away from him. "We're going to pretend I never said that."

"Bien sûr."

There was a beat of silence before Toby chuckled.

Then he groaned as well. "Ow. Don't make me laugh," he mumbled.

Gideon fell back asleep with a smile, albeit short-lived . . . until his next bathroom visit.

THE NEXT TIME HE OPENED HIS EYES, TOBY WAS pressed against his back again. It wasn't sexual, or even affectionate. It was just pure comfort. He knew most people wanted to be left alone when they were sick, but he'd always needed comfort and apparently Toby did too.

Gideon was reluctant to move. He wanted to stay there with Toby against him for the longest time, but Gideon's whole body ached. He'd been lying down for too long, he wanted a shower, and to brush his teeth.

But first, he needed to see Benson.

He peeled himself away from Toby so as not to wake him, then sat on the edge of the bed to test his stomach. It felt marginally better.

He sipped the flat, warm Lucozade and gave it a second to settle in his belly before he stood up. He walked gingerly out to the living room. All the lights were off, the house was quiet.

He hadn't realised it was dark outside.

God, what time is it?

Going back down the hall, he saw the other bedroom door was open and spotted a sleeping Carla in bed. He couldn't believe Toby's mum was sleeping here so she could look after Benson.

He felt guilty that she'd been inconvenienced, but he was so very grateful.

And if he were being honest with himself, he also felt something else. Longing, he wished his own mother was here. Wishing he could call her like Toby called his mum.

And he felt comforted knowing he wasn't alone.

Sure, Carla was Toby's support team, but that didn't diminish the glow of warmth any. She'd cared for Benson like one of her own, and that made Gideon's heart swell.

He checked on Benson next. Safe and sound asleep in his crib, in his puppy pyjamas.

God, Gideon missed him.

It'd only been one full day, and he'd been in the house with him the whole time. It wasn't like they'd been separated or torn apart. But not being part of Benson's day made Gideon feel inadequate, like a bad parent.

Sick or not.

He stood there staring at him, watching him breathe, peaceful and loved, until his body reminded him of the day he'd had. He'd been upright for too long. Five minutes was too much, apparently.

Heavy and achy, still unwell and miserable, he went back to bed.

"Hmm okay?" Toby asked sleepily.

"Yeah," Gideon mumbled. "Your mum's an angel."

———

When he woke up next, he was spooning Toby; his arm draped over his mid-section, his knee pressed against Toby's leg, and face against his shoulder blade. He knew it was wrong to be cuddling him, to even touch him while he was sleeping, even if Gideon had been asleep when he'd done it.

But man, it felt so right.

Until Toby rolled over in his arms and snuggled into him. Gideon froze, unsure of what to do, but then Toby mumbled something in his sleep, disgruntled and whiney.

So Gideon lowered his arm and exhaled slowly. As soon as Gideon was holding him, Toby relaxed and his soft snores made Gideon smile.

Was this even happening?

How were they going to talk about this in the light of day? Would they even mention it at all?

He wasn't sure. Though if he did, he might get a better idea of what their relationship actually was. Would Toby be horrified and laugh it off? Or would he admit to being as confused as Gideon?

Gideon had no way of knowing. The last day had been straight from the depths of hell, and it had put them in a strange position.

Either way, things would be different. And the likelihood of Gideon lying in bed with Toby in his arms any time soon would be pretty slim. So as wrong as it might have been, for as right as it felt, Gideon held him a little tighter.

Toby woke up in Gideon's bed. He was alone, the room quiet, the lights off. *Gideon must be with Benson . . .*

Toby sat up, his body sore and his stomach tender and raw. But he remembered the touch, the warmth and reassurance of being in bed with Gideon.

It felt like a feverish dream, but he recalled waking a few times and finding himself the big spoon. Then the next time he was the little spoon. He was pretty sure he woke up at one point with his head on Gideon's chest, Gideon's arm around his shoulder.

He was sure he hadn't dreamt it. Did he want it to be a dream? Or did he want it to be real?

Don't be stupid, Toby.

He shook his head and went to the en suite bathroom, but as soon as he reached for the door handle, Gideon came out in a billow of steam and almost collected him.

He was wearing nothing but a towel, his hair wet, beads of water running enviable lines down his skin.

"Oh," Gideon said.

"Shit, sorry," Toby said. "I didn't hear you in there." He was trying very hard not to look . . . at his chest, his stomach, the towel tied at his waist, the bulge it tried to hide. "Um . . ."

Gideon smirked at him. "Feeling better?"

Toby had to think. "Uh."

"Have a hot shower," Gideon said. "It will make you feel a hundred times better."

"Yes. Shower." He nodded, like an idiot.

Gideon was still very much almost-naked, still wet, still really close.

Still gorgeous.

Toby took a step backward. "Shower. Good idea," he mumbled. Then, turning on his heel, he made a break for his own bathroom.

He took a second to catch his breath.

He caught a glimpse of himself in the mirror. The food poisoning had done a number on him. He was pale, had dark smudges under his eyes, and he'd definitely lost some weight. But in his eyes was a troubled man. A man who knew he'd crossed a line.

He hadn't done anything with Gideon, except for sharing a bed and waking up intermittently with their bodies entwined. Not that it had been deliberate . . . So no, Toby hadn't done anything with Gideon.

But he wanted to.

His mum had stripped his bed and shoved him into Gideon's room, into his bed, in that no-nonsense way his mother had. "You need to rest," she'd said. "I will clean this up, remake it, and I will sleep in here to look after Benson."

And Toby had been too ill to argue. Too ill to care.

He'd just wanted to lie down.

And then, because he'd been upright for too long, he'd needed to vomit. Again. And after that, he'd come out of Gideon's en suite, climbed into the bed where his mother had insisted he sleep, and he'd slept.

It was only now that it was dawning on him how much of a bad idea that had been.

Because Gideon felt good in his arms. With gentle back rubs and comforting arms.

Goddammit.

Toby made the shower as hot as he could stand it, hoping it would wash away the gross, sick feeling, but also hoping it would clear his head and make him see reason.

Of course it didn't.

Well, he did feel better, yes.

But he still wanted to shag his boss.

He couldn't make eye contact with himself in the mirror as he dried off. Mad at himself, he threw on some trackies and a T-shirt and went to face the music.

Gideon was sitting on the floor, his back against the couch, with Benson on his lap. Benson gave Toby a big smile with loud babbling.

Toby didn't know which of them was cuter.

He sat on the couch with a sigh as his mum came out from the kitchen, holding a coffee mug. "Oh Toby, you're here. I made some tea for you both." She put the mug on the table beside the couch, took Benson, and popped him in his bouncer. "Black tea with sugar for you, Gideon." She nodded to where she'd put the mug.

Gideon got himself up slowly and sat on the couch. "I can see where you get your bossiness from," he said to Toby. He picked up the tea and frowned at it. "I don't think I can drink this."

"It'll help fix you up," Carla said as she came out with a second mug and handed it to Toby. "Here you go."

"Thanks, Mum."

"Think you're up for some plain toast?" she asked.

They both shook their heads. Toby tried the tea. All his life, whenever he was ill and starting to feel better, his mum made him black tea with sugar and plain toast with butter. Sometimes it was like choking down cardboard. Sometimes it tasted like heaven.

But it always made him feel a bit better.

"I'll just strip your bed," Carla said, walking to the hall. "Make it fresh for you." She stopped at the door and turned to Gideon. "Any favourite sheet sets from the linen cupboard?"

He shook his head. "Mrs Barlow, you don't need to do that."

"Nonsense, dear." She disappeared down the hall. "And call me Carla. Mrs Barlow is my mother-in-law."

"It's easier not to argue," Toby suggested.

Gideon groaned. "She's already done so much."

"She loves fussing over people. It's her drug of choice. I mean it. She'll be offended if you tell her not to fuss over you. Especially when you're sick. She goes into boss-mum mode. It's why I called her."

Gideon gave Toby half a smile. "I'm so glad you did." Then he glanced over at Benson. "I don't know what I would have done. It's the hardest part about being a single parent with no family," he said quietly. "There's no one to call."

Toby's heart squeezed at the sadness on Gideon's face. He hated that this was his reality. "Well," he offered gently, "you're not alone anymore. You've got me, and my mother, who was raised by her Italian grandmother, who will fuss over you and Benson until it hurts."

Gideon's gaze met his, and there was a profound sadness in his eyes that Toby hadn't expected. "Thank you," he murmured.

They watched Benson for a bit, then Gideon smiled his way. "What did you do in London when you were sick and couldn't call your mum to come over?"

"Well, I never gave anyone food poisoning in London," Toby replied. "I really am so very sorry about that. I'm never making sticky chicken again. Or any chicken, for that matter."

Gideon grimaced at the mention of chicken. He put his cup of tea back on the side table. "Yeah, I'm not ready for tea yet."

Toby put his down too. "Me either."

"Not sure how I can still be tired," Gideon mumbled.

Carla came back out to the living room. "Okay, so both beds are clean and remade. Hope it wasn't too uncomfortable having to share a bed last night."

Toby and Gideon both looked at each other, and Toby could feel his cheeks burning. The tops of Gideon's ears went red.

"Washing machine's going, and the dryer," Carla added, oblivious to the awkwardness she'd just bestowed upon them. She checked her watch. "Your dad'll be here any minute to pick me up. I have to drop him off at the bowling club. He has his game. You know how he is."

Wait . . . Toby looked out the window as if he could read the daylight like a clock. "What time is it?"

"Almost four."

"Four?" He couldn't believe it. "Oh my god. Did we sleep all that time?"

Gideon gave a nod. "Apparently. And I'm ready to go back to bed."

"Toby, dear, what are you doing?" his mum asked. "Did you want to come home with us? It *is* Saturday. It's technically your weekend off, and I can't stay tonight."

Saturday?

Toby squinted at her. "What the hell happened to Friday?"

"You spent it facing alternate ends at the toilet," she replied. "Mostly."

He sunk back in the couch. "Mum. That's gross."

Gideon snorted.

He'd missed a whole day? It was almost Saturday night, which meant he'd only have to be back again tomorrow. He let out a sigh. "The thought of getting into a car right now . . ." He shook his head. "I can't. I want to stay right here on this couch, watch some rubbish movie, and not move all day tomorrow either. Sorry, Mum."

"Oh, don't worry," she said, waving him off. "You don't need to explain, love. I still got to see you, and I got to spend time with this cutest little jelly bean." She went to Benson and made his favourite toy caterpillar give him kisses, making him giggle and gurgle. A car honked out on the street, so Carla stood up, grabbed her bag, and went to the door. "There's more Lucozade in the fridge. Both of you drink some if you can't drink the tea. You must stay hydrated. And make sure you have tea and toast in the morning. Toby, I'll call to check on you. Gideon, you feel better soon, okay? And look after your precious boy."

Gideon smiled. "I will. Thank you so much, for everything. You're a life saver, and I'm forever indebted to you."

"I'll take payment in more cuddles with Benson when you're feeling better," she said. Then with a wave, she was out the door and gone.

They were both quiet for a bit, then Toby shot Gideon a look. "She'll hold you to that payment," he said. "In full. With interest."

Gideon chuckled, clearly tired. "I'm sure Benson won't mind." He pulled the rocker closer and handed the caterpillar back to Benson. Or maybe just to be closer to Benson, Toby wasn't sure. "Your mum really saved my arse."

"She saved both our arses," Toby amended. "She helped me too. I was supposed to mind Benson all day yesterday." He sighed. "I can't believe today's Saturday. And it's almost over, apparently." He looked around and shrugged. "I don't even know where my phone is."

"And you didn't have to stay . . . though I do appreciate it."

Toby liked that Gideon wanted him around, but he had to be honest. "Well, I figure it'll take both of us to look after Benson tonight and tomorrow. But truthfully, I wasn't kidding about the idea of getting into a car right now makes me feel ill. And I'd have to put up with Josh being loud and wanting me to do stuff . . ." The corner of his mouth pulled down. "Staying here where it's quiet and not a whole houseful of people, where it's just us three, watching trashy

TV shows and not getting off this couch for a whole day? Sounds good to me."

Gideon's eyes met his. "Sounds good to me too."

THEY SPENT THE NEXT TWENTY-FOUR HOURS DOING exactly that. They made sure Benson was fed, clean, cuddled, and happy, and they spent all day Sunday on the couches with blankets watching stupid reality shows. They hadn't shared a bed again, even though Toby had wanted to.

"I'll just have to suffer alone," Toby had joked at his bedroom door on the Saturday night. "No cuddle buddy. It almost made food poisoning worth it."

He'd thrown out the bait, but Gideon, although he looked somewhat stunned, didn't bite.

"Just kidding," Toby had added, trying to play it off. He'd meant it as a joke, but not really. "Nothing is worth food poisoning. Good night."

He'd closed the door and stopped just short of banging his head on it.

Stupid thing to say, Toby.

On Sunday night, after Benson was bathed, fed, and in his bed, Gideon and Toby were on the couch watching their baking show and sipping on black tea. They had managed to keep down some toast during the day, but neither of them wanted to risk more than tea, more Lucozade, and some saltine crackers.

They were on the same couch, at either ends, though sharing a blanket. Not that it was cold, it was more of a comfort thing.

"I'm so wiped," Toby admitted. "We've done nothing for days, but god, I'm still so tired."

"Yeah, I won't be far out of bed tonight, I don't think," Gideon replied.

"If Benson wakes during the night," Toby said, "I'll get up with him. You have to go into work tomorrow. Driving, walking, sitting in an office." Toby made a face. "You need more sleep than me. I can spend most of my day in this very spot tomorrow. Might brave the park if the weather's okay. Not sure if the sun will fix me or kill me, but I think Benson needs more than just a walk around the backyard. I'll see how I'm feeling tomorrow. I didn't sleep too well last night."

"Me either," Gideon said. "Maybe we slept ourselves out."

Toby agreed. "I still don't know what the hell happened to Friday. Feels like there's a glitch in the matrix or we crossed the Date Line or something. We missed a whole day."

Gideon chuckled. "Having a cuddle buddy to sleep with, right? Best sleep ever."

"Oh my god, I know, right?" Toby thought it was a bit weird that Gideon was bringing it up, considering he'd baulked in the hall the night before when Toby had mentioned it. Toby guessed Gideon was more comfortable now he'd had a whole day to think about it. "I've always been that way, though. Sleep better with someone beside me, that is. And just sleeping. No funny business."

The corner of Gideon's lip curved upward. "Same."

They were both quiet for a bit, Toby pretending to watch TV while his mind scrambled for something to say . . . but Gideon beat him to it.

"Can we talk about that?" he asked. "About what happened. Not that anything happened, but I just feel we should talk about the fact you slept in my bed. While I was in it. And there are employment stipulations and complications, and I just think we should clear the air."

Gideon had his serious face on, with his professional voice, and Toby was sure he was about to hear bad news.

His mouth went dry, his heart was in his throat.

And his stomach sank to the floor.

Chapter Ten

"You what?"

Lauren's voice cranked up an octave. They were having a quick lunch in a café around the corner from his work. Well, Lauren was eating a whole bowl of pasta. Gideon was having some crackers and apple juice. "Gideon, oh my god."

He sighed. "I know."

"Tell me everything."

"Well, it started with undercooked chicken."

"I don't want to know the gross parts. You shared a bed when you were both sick as dogs, and that's kinda weird. How can you want anyone near you when you're sick like that?"

"I just find it comforting."

"And you woke up several times to find yourself either hugging him or being hugged by him."

"Correct."

"And you said *what* to him last night?"

"Well, he'd joked about it on Saturday night first, but in a not-joking way, if you know what I mean. So technically, *he* brought it up first. And I was too stunned to reply. I wasn't expecting him to joke about being cuddle buddies. I'd never even heard of that before."

"But then you asked him to be a cuddle buddy last night?"

Gideon winced with a nod. "He said he sleeps better. I said I do too. I told him if he wasn't comfortable because of the work-slash-boss situation, I would completely understand. He smiled like he wanted to. You know when someone's eyes light up?" Lauren nodded. "But then he said he probably shouldn't. And I understood. I mean, one of us was being reasonable and sensible. And it wasn't me."

"And then what happened?"

"We went to bed. Separately," Gideon said. "And ten minutes later he knocked on my door, told me to shut up, and got into my bed."

"What did you do?"

"I laughed."

"No." She shook her head. "When he got into your bed, what did you do?"

"We went to sleep."

"Sleep?"

"Like a baby. Which is a stupid saying, because I can tell you, babies don't sleep that well."

Lauren was staring at him, her pasta forgotten. "Gideon. Details, please. How was it this morning? Any awkwardness?"

"Nope. He made me tea. I made him toast."

"Jesus. Are you married already?"

He chuckled. "There was no hugging last night in bed. No waking up wrapped around each other."

"You sound disappointed."

He didn't even try to deny it. "I should feel bad for asking him if he wanted to sleep in my bed. I am technically his boss. But I don't regret it, Lauren. I just don't. He's a great guy, and I like him. Is it complicated? Yes. Could it all go horribly wrong? Yes." He shrugged. "Was I worried about that before? Yes."

"You're not worried about that now?"

He shook his head, then shrugged. "I don't know. If he left, I'd be devastated. And not just because he's a great nanny. I'd miss . . . him."

She frowned with a sigh.

"We haven't done anything. There's no sex involved," Gideon added, as if that made a difference.

"But you wouldn't say no."

His eyes met hers. "No. I wouldn't. But we'd need to discuss that, and it would have to be his decision, not mine."

She took a mouthful and chewed thoughtfully.

"We'd already shared a bed once, thanks to his mum. It was her doing," he said, and Lauren's eyes went wide. He waved her off. "That's a long story and, mind you, Toby and I shared a horrible forty-something hours. It wasn't pretty. And I guess since we endured disgusting bodily functions together, we're even closer. Yesterday, we spent all day vegging out on the couch, helping each other look after Benson."

Like a couple would . . .

She nodded to his lunch of crackers and juice. "And you're still not feeling better?"

"I feel much better than I was, but I'm not game to test my stomach."

Just then, his phone rang with his usual lunchtime Face-Time. Gideon rested the phone up against the window at the end of the table so they could both see the screen. He answered the call and Benson's smiling face filled the screen.

"Say hello to Dadda," Toby's voice said. "And tell Dadda you had a bottle *and* some Farex because you're a big boy." Then there was a beat of silence. "Oh, you're not in your office. Sorry."

Lauren leaned in so her face was on screen. "Hi, Toby! We're at lunch."

Then Toby's face was on screen, smiling. Beautiful. "Oh hey," he replied. Then he propped the phone up, scooped up Benson, and sat him on his knee. He faced Benson toward the screen. "Look, he's in his orange spaceman outfit today. Isn't he just the cutest astronaut you've ever seen?"

Gideon nodded. "Sure is."

He wasn't just talking about Benson. And he could feel Lauren's eyes on him, but he refused to glance at her.

"We're going to brave the park this arvo," Toby said. "I think I'm up for it. I had crackers for lunch and some Lucozade, and I feel much better."

Gideon held up his crackers and juice. "Same."

Toby smiled and gave Benson a kiss on the top of his head. It made Gideon's heart thump.

"I might make a soup for dinner, with just vegetables and stock," Toby said. He leaned in closer to the camera. "No chicken."

Gideon chuckled. "Sounds perfect."

Then Toby waved Benson's little hand. "Say bye-bye to Dadda. If we're going to the park, we need to get going."

Gideon smiled fondly at the screen and waved. "Bye."

Lauren waved too. "Bye!"

As soon as the screen was black, she shoved Gideon gently. "You're done for."

He scoffed. "What?"

"The way you look at him."

"I was looking at Benson."

She raised a don't-bullshit-me eyebrow. "No, you had an 'awwww, there's my cute boy' look on your face when Benson was on screen, but when it was Toby, and Toby holding Benson, your whole face changed. Gideon, I know you."

He was going to argue . . . but what was the point?

Lauren took one last mouthful of pasta before pushing it away. "What are you going to do?"

"About what?"

"About him."

"Nothing. I'm going to continue having dinner with him every night, watch TV, and take the piss out of all the stupid reality show people. And sleep next to him in the same bed, if he wants to continue doing that, and make him toast in the mornings, and have video calls every day at lunchtime."

"You're basically a couple," she said. "Without the official commitment. And that's going to lead to hurt feelings. I'm only saying this because I love you, but I think it might be your heart that gets broken, and I don't want that for you."

"I don't want that either."

"I think maybe you and Toby need to have a little chat."

Gideon sighed.

He hated that she was right.

"I know."

"Don't forget you're technically his boss."

Gideon cringed. "There's no way to make this right. If he is interested in me, what does that mean for his job as a nanny? For his job with us? I don't want to lose him as a nanny. He's slotted into our lives so perfectly. And his mum was so great. She looked after us, and she fussed over me."

He couldn't believe he was going to admit this out loud. "It was so nice to have a mum fuss over me. I've missed that."

Lauren made a sad face. "Oh, Gideon."

"And I know this just all makes me sound pathetic, but I like that I'm not alone anymore. I like the comfort of having Toby around, asleep next to me. I like that his mum totally fucking babied me when I was ill." He shrugged. "But it's more than that."

"I know it is," she said gently. "I saw your face just now when you saw him. I saw the look in your eyes."

His stomach felt all tight, and it had nothing to do with food poisoning. "So I think I'll do and say nothing. I'll enjoy our nights together, the dinners, the company, the laughs, without risking pushing him away. And if things between us change, if things progress—" He gave her a look and she understood what that meant. "—then we can deal with it. But until then . . ."

She patted his arm. "Until then."

Toby sat down next to Anika, Benson on his lap.

"Oh my god, have you lost five kilos since last week?" she asked.

"Not quite five," he said.

"Tell me how," she begged, poking her tummy. "Three babies have done this to me."

"Um, undercooked chicken," he replied. "And three days of wanting to die."

"Eww." She made a face. "That's not good."

He shook his head. "Nope. It wasn't. We just started to come good yesterday afternoon."

"We?"

"Me and Gideon."

She tweaked Benson's chubby leg. "Not this little angel?"

"Oh goodness, no. Thank god food poisoning's not contagious."

"I'm glad you're feeling better." Then she did a weird thing with her eyebrow. "So how is your sexy boss with his sexy moustache? Still sexy?"

"As ever."

She seemed surprised by this. "Oh?" She leaned in and whispered, "Just how sexy are we talking?"

Toby chuckled, but he clearly remembered Gideon coming out of his bathroom with just a towel around his waist, water beaded on his skin. And how he looked in his suit pants and business shirt this morning.

He sighed. "You know, I never had a thing for moustaches before now."

She grinned. "You know they call them 'handlebar moustaches' for a reason—so you've got something to hold on to."

"Oh my god!" Toby covered Benson's ears.

Anika laughed, but she waved him off. "My bestie is gay," she whispered. "And TMI is his middle name. He tells me everything, and I do mean *ev-er-y*-thing."

Toby snorted. "Well, as sexy as he is, we're not . . . holding onto moustaches, if you know what I mean." He sighed. "He is my boss, after all."

She made a face. "You know what I say? To hell with the rules. If it's good and you want it, go for it. You're consenting adults, and life's too short."

"It's not that simple," he grumbled. "I'm technically through an agency. If they found out . . ."

"Who's gonna tell them?"

He laughed and shook his head. "It doesn't matter anyway. He's not interested. And *I'm* not interested either! What am I saying? I'm talking like I'm interested, and I'm not. I'm really not."

Anika raised one perfectly arched eyebrow. "Mm-hmm. Just so you know, if you ever get kidnapped and need to lie to save your life, you're one hundred percent dead. You're not even surviving a little bit. That was woeful."

He nudged his shoulder to hers. "Thanks." He had to use Benson's bib to wipe the rivers of drool from his chin, then he gave him a gel teething ring.

"Ugh, teething is the worst," Anika said. "Oh, that reminds me, I have a voucher for nappies." She rifled through her nappy bag and handed Toby a slip of paper. "Too small for my Mister Chonkus here," she said, giving her gorgeous little one a kiss.

"Oh, thank you so much! Anything I can use to save Gideon some money would be great."

"Tell me about it," she said. "I have to go back to work in two months. Nine weeks to be exact." She looked at Malek fondly. "I wanted to have longer, but money's getting tight. Maternity leave was great while it lasted." She sighed. "But I'm luckier than some; I have my old job to go back to and I earn good money at work, so I can't really complain about that. I just wish I could stay home with them forever, ya know?"

Toby nodded. "Gideon struggled with it too. But we FaceTime him during his lunch break, which helps, I think. Have you thought about childcare options?"

Anika made a face and sighed again. "There's a crèche in my office building . . ."

"But?" There was definitely a *but* coming.

"But I don't know. It's convenient, yes. But I don't know

if it's right for us. I've met with them and they're all lovely and professional, but . . ." She met Toby's gaze. "God, I'm going to be one of those kinds of parents, aren't I? The 'my babies are too precious for anything generic' bullshit I used to hate. I used to make fun of people like me, Toby."

He laughed, but he understood her dilemma. "You gotta do what's right for you and for your babies. No childcare situation is perfect."

"Except yours," she said with another nudge against Toby's shoulder. "Being a live-in nanny for Mr Hottie Biscottie."

Toby chuckled, but Benson began to grumble. Toby pulled him onto his lap, gave him cuddles, tried to make him laugh, but it was to no avail. "Okay, I better get this one home for a nap."

Anika made a sad face. "Aww, I hope his teeth come through soon."

Toby groaned. "God, me too." He packed up and walked home, and Benson grumbled most of the afternoon. He didn't sleep much and even the teething gel didn't help. He was crying when Gideon got home. He came straight into the kitchen where Toby was trying to distract Benson with getting some dinner ready. "Oh, what's wrong with my little man?"

"He needs Dadda cuddles," Toby said as an explanation, handing Benson over to him. "It makes his gums feel better."

Toby was sure Gideon's cuddles could fix anything. He distinctly remembered his arms around him and exactly how that felt . . . and how much he'd like to feel that again.

As soon as Gideon held Benson, Benson burrowed his face into Gideon's neck and stopped crying. Gideon's face was priceless. "Aww."

"I told you he needed his dadda."

He smiled, rubbing Benson's back, swaying a little. "Is it just teeth do you think?"

Toby nodded. "Yeah. If you see his gums, you can see his teeth are right there."

Gideon kept rubbing Benson's back and frowned. "Poor little guy."

"I've got soup on. Still sound good?"

Gideon nodded. "Perfect."

"Go and sit down with him and I'll finish up in here."

"Are you sure?"

"Absolutely. I think Benson's sick of looking at my face today anyway. He definitely needs Dadda cuddles."

Gideon made a pouty sad face. "I highly doubt he's sick of your face," he said, still rubbing Benson's back. "You have one of his favourite faces."

Toby smiled as he watched Gideon walk out of the kitchen. He loved seeing Gideon with Benson. It made him so happy to just see them together. It had always made Toby pleased to see the kids he cared for bonding with their parents.

Yet this felt different somehow.

Maybe it was because Gideon was a single dad. A single gay dad, at that.

But the way it made his whole chest warm and the butterflies in his belly jittery and lovely . . . he'd never felt like this about any family he'd worked with.

He wasn't sure if he'd felt this way about anyone.

Stirring the soup for longer than necessary, he gave Gideon some alone time with Benson, and to also give his heart a moment to breathe.

He knew his feelings for Gideon weren't conducive to a

working relationship, so he tried to ignore it. He ignored it when he went back into the lounge room and found Gideon holding a sleepy Benson, gently rocking him, caressing his cheek.

He ignored it when they ate their soup, sitting across from each other at the table. He ignored the way Gideon smiled, eyes shining when he looked at him.

He ignored the swoop of his belly, the clutch of his heart.

He ignored the way his whole chest thrummed when Gideon sang to Benson when he bathed him, fed him, and put him to bed.

"Love you to the moon and back," Gideon sang, his made-up lullaby, soft and soothing.

Toby ignored that the most.

He ignored how Gideon chose the same sofa as Toby to sit on, leg curled up underneath him, sitting a little closer than he probably had to. Toby ignored the flood of butter-flies that gave him.

He ignored the way his heart hammered when Gideon made him a cup of tea, and he ignored how he sat even closer than he had before.

At bedtime, Toby opted to sleep in his own bed. For the sake of his sanity. For his job.

He ignored the flinch of Gideon's eyes, the way he tried to hide his surprise and hurt. He lay there, staring at his ceiling for what felt like hours, any hopes of sleep long gone, replaced with images of Gideon's smile, his eyes, his mous-tache. The warmth and surety of every brush of fingers, the way that made Toby feel.

He wanted to know what he felt like against him. He wanted to know what he kissed like. God, what he would do to know how Gideon kissed. Toby was sure Gideon would be a great kisser. He wanted to know what that moustache felt like . . .

Stop thinking about it, Toby, and go to sleep.

But he had no hope of sleeping at all. And just after one o'clock in the morning, he sat on the edge of his bed in the dark, mad at himself for what he was about to do.

He snatched up his pillow and yanked back his bedroom door, fully intending to go into Gideon's room. But Gideon's door was open and the kitchen light was on. And was that a tap running?

Was he not feeling well?

Oh god, had Toby food poisoned him twice in a week?

He went toward the kitchen and found Gideon at the sink, drinking a glass of water. He wore his blue striped pyjama pants and a white tee. He didn't seem surprised to see Toby, and he didn't appear ill.

He looked Toby up and down, pausing at the pillow Toby was holding.

"Couldn't sleep," Toby said.

"Same," Gideon murmured. He held the glass out. "Do you want some water?"

Toby walked close enough to take the glass. He gulped it, his eyes on Gideon, and he watched as Gideon's eyes dropped to his mouth and his throat as he swallowed. Gideon's lips parted when Toby's tongue caught an errant bead of water, his gaze fixed and heated.

Holy shit.

For all the ignoring he'd done, for all the pretending he'd managed, Toby couldn't ignore that.

Gideon took the glass, their fingers brushing again, hot and electric.

Gideon let out a sharp breath and his gaze flashed to

Toby's. "I, um, I should . . ." He swallowed hard, his chest rising and falling. "God, I need to—"

He went to step around Toby, but Toby grabbed his arm. He hadn't meant to. He had no recollection of moving, but when he looked down, his hand had a hold of Gideon.

Gideon looked down at Toby's hand, then up to his face, his eyes imploring, his lips parted, chest heaving.

They were so close, their bodies almost touching. The heat between them ready to combust.

Toby dropped his pillow and slid his hand along Gideon's jaw, feeling the stubble over heated skin. Those pink lips almost did his head in, and if he didn't kiss them, feel them and taste them, Toby was sure he'd lose his mind.

He leaned in, lifted Gideon's jaw a little, their noses barely an inch apart. Gideon gasped, and he licked his lips.

"Tell me yes," Toby breathed.

Gideon slow blinked, his eyes dark. "Yes."

Thank god.

Toby crushed his mouth to Gideon's, hard and demanding. Pushing Gideon against the kitchen counter, Toby slid his tongue into Gideon's mouth.

He'd wanted this for too long to be patient or gentle.

Gideon grunted as their tongues met, and the sound made Toby's knees weak. His fingers found Gideon's hair, holding his head, kissing him deeper, harder. He tasted like mint and dreams come true.

Gideon wrapped his arms around Toby, pulling him close, and Toby could feel Gideon's arousal pressing against his own.

It made Gideon groan and grind against him, his hands gliding down over Toby's arse, squeezing, pulling him closer still.

Tongues, teeth, hands, and body heat, everything Toby

needed. Gideon's hold on him tightened, and Gideon pushed against him, turning him around and pushing him harder against the counter. Desperate, demanding . . .

Toby still held Gideon's face, his neck, still had his tongue in Gideon's mouth, and he had to make a decision . . .

Simmer down or take it to bed.

With his hands cupping Gideon's face, he broke the kiss, their foreheads touching. Breaths ragged, chests heaving. "Tell me what to do," Toby whispered.

Gideon's eyes closed and he looked torn. But their hips were still flush together, erections pressed between them.

But there was no answer.

"It's okay," he murmured, taking a step back.

Gideon reached out and snatched a fistful of Toby's shirt. And when Gideon looked at him, even in the darkened kitchen, fire burned in Gideon's eyes.

That was all the answer Toby needed.

Chapter Eleven

GIDEON KNEW THERE WAS NO GOING BACK.

In hindsight, he knew there was no going back from the moment he admitted to himself that he had feelings for Toby.

But to kiss him?

To taste him, and feel his body, and hold him?

He'd crossed the line, and he wasn't sorry. He wanted this. He wanted Toby more than he'd ever wanted anyone else, and now that he'd had a taste . . .

He hadn't meant to grab Toby's shirt like that, but the idea of him walking away made Gideon's body react.

"I want you," Gideon said, his voice rough. "But I have to know if you're okay with that. I know it's complicated, but fuck, Toby, I want you. I want you in my bed, not just to sleep. I want to be with you. But I need you to tell me you want this."

Toby peeled Gideon's fingers from his shirt and, still holding his hand, led him to Gideon's room. Gideon's heart was in his throat, thundering. And to Gideon's surprise,

Toby pulled Gideon's shirt off and pushed him onto the bed.

He climbed on after him, crawling up his body, his eyes fierce and determined. He pulled his own shirt off then and threw it to the floor. "I'm more than okay with it," he said, crashing his mouth to Gideon's, forcing his tongue inside.

Toby's knees widened Gideon's legs and he lowered his body onto Gideon's, Toby's erection hot and hard against his own. Gideon gasped, his hips rising up, grinding, gripping him, desperate for more.

Toby was completely in charge of him, and Gideon surrendered. The pleasure, the desire, being wanted like this.

All Gideon could do was groan and give Toby whatever he wanted.

And Toby had no qualms in taking it.

The perfect mix of demanding and gentle, he held him, fingers digging into his skin, then featherlight touches. His tongue delved deep, then he sucked on Gideon's bottom lip. He kissed down Gideon's neck, soft and sweet, then scraped his teeth and nipped. He groaned filthy nothings in his ear, then whined like a virgin.

Gideon's whole body was on fire. Every cell at the mercy of Toby's touch. He was close to coming already. And then Toby leaned back, palming Gideon's cock, slipping his hand into his briefs to wrap his fingers around him.

Slick with precome, the slide was wet and hot, the pleasure too much.

"Fuck, Toby, oh god," Gideon gasped. His cock was rock hard, his orgasm so close, pushing him to that place where pain and pleasure meet. "Gonna come."

"Yeah, give it to me," Toby grunted.

Ecstasy crashed over Gideon, a blinding pleasure

exploded within him, and he spilled over the edge. His back arched off the bed and he shot his load onto his belly, over Toby's hand. His orgasm rolled through him, wave after wave, his mind blessedly wiped blank.

He barely even noticed Toby leaning over him, one hand near Gideon's head, the other stroking his own cock. Gideon tried to focus on the cockhead sliding through Toby's fist, but Toby's face . . . the pleasure and urgency was a true thing of beauty.

Gideon reached down and cupped Toby's balls, and Toby's eyes shot open, and with a loud moan, he shot his load onto Gideon's chest.

"So fucking hot."

Toby shuddered as he squeezed the last of his come out, dropping his head down, panting and spent.

Gideon pulled him down, taking his full weight and not even caring about the mess between them.

"That was the hottest hand job ever," Gideon murmured, and Toby chuckled.

He sounded exhausted and he was a dead weight on top of Gideon. A delicious, perfect weight. He traced circles on Toby's back, patterns and swirls. He almost hoped Toby would fall asleep, that they could stay like that all night.

Where reality wouldn't ever bother them.

With a sigh, Gideon rolled them onto their sides. "Let me get a washcloth."

Toby mumbled but didn't open his eyes, so Gideon slipped out of bed. He cleaned himself up, changed into some clean boxer pants, and took a wet washcloth back to the bed.

Toby was on his back, eyes shut, breaths even and deep. It made Gideon smile . . . He wiped him down and tossed the towel toward the en suite door, then pulled Toby into his arms.

Things would be different come morning.

Gideon didn't know if they'd be better or worse, but he knew without a doubt their relationship had changed.

So if all he had was this night, this right here with Toby in his arms, the smell of their sex on their skin, then Gideon would take it. Toby snuggled into him, breathing deep. Gideon tightened his hold, kissed the top of his head, and closed his eyes.

GIDEON WOKE UP ALONE.

It wasn't unusual. Toby often got up before him, tending to Benson.

But last night had been different.

Had Toby needed some distance? Had he woken up with regrets?

Gideon sure as hell hoped not. He strained to listen, to hear what, exactly, he wasn't sure. But he heard nothing.

He had to get up and face the music. He and Toby would need to talk, that much was clear.

Just as he was about to throw back the covers, his bedroom door swung inward and Toby appeared, holding Benson like a little Superman, flying him into the room.

"Look, Dadda," Toby said, smiling wide. "Look who got two teeth!"

Gideon sat up. "He did?"

"Yep." Toby handed Benson to him. Benson was smiling, drooling, but sure enough there were two little white bottom teeth.

Gideon couldn't believe it! "Look at them! Who's a big

boy now?" He blew raspberries on Benson's tummy and on his neck, making Benson squeal and laugh.

When Gideon looked up at Toby, Toby was staring at him, eyes wide. "Oh."

He stopped, his stomach dropping. "Oh, what?"

Toby rubbed his own neck and frowned. "Ah, you're gonna have to wear a tie to work today. Is it too hot for a turtleneck?" The corner of his lip drew down. "Sorry."

Oh.

Toby put one knee on the bed, leaned over, and took Benson. "This little chicky nuggy needs more breakfast." Then he looked at Gideon's neck again and grimaced, but also kind of laughed. "Sorry about that."

Well, so much for any awkwardness.

Gideon rolled out of bed and went to his bathroom to take a piss and to see what the hell was wrong with his neck . . .

Holy shit.

A big purple hickey was splotched on the side of his throat, down to where his shoulder started.

He remembered the way Toby had scraped his teeth there, how he'd sucked and licked. He remembered how good it had felt.

But holy hell, he looked like he'd been in a plum fight, and lost.

He doubted a collared shirt and tie would even hide it.

Gideon leaned in closer to inspect it. Were those teeth marks? Sure looked like it.

But he caught himself smiling as he skimmed his fingers over the purple blotch, and he met his own gaze in the reflection. Did he regret what they'd done? Absolutely not. Did he care that he had a huge purple love-bite on his neck? Hell no.

129

Actually, he liked it.

He liked that Toby had done that, marked him.

He relieved himself, and washing his hands caught himself still smiling in the mirror.

Get a grip, Gideon.

Shaking his head at himself, he went in search of coffee and a certain little chicky nuggy with two teeth.

Did I just call him chicky nuggy?

God help me.

Benson was in his bouncer, parked in front of the sofa, and Toby was feeding him a spoonful of runny Farex. It looked incredibly unappetising to Gideon, but Benson was clearly enjoying it.

"I can't believe he has two teeth," Gideon said.

"I can't believe I did that to you," Toby said, pointing the spoon to Gideon's neck. "Do you bruise easily? Or was I just a bit too eager?"

Right. So we were just going to talk about it openly like this.

"Well, I've never been one to bruise easily before, so . . ."

"So I was too eager? Is that what you're saying?"

Jeez.

"Uh, I'd say you were the right amount of eager. If eager was a quantifiable thing, you were definitely the perfect amount."

Toby laughed as he stood up. "Are you embarrassed?"

"No, I just . . . I wasn't sure how we'd *be* this morning. If you know what I mean."

Toby handed him the bowl of Farex. "I'll go make the coffee. You feed this little Hungry Hippo and check out his new chompers."

So apparently how they would *be* with each other this morning was exactly how they were every morning.

Gideon smiled, relieved. *Soooo relieved.*

He took a seat and began feeding Benson, catching a glimpse every so often of those two tiny white teeth that had troubled him for weeks. Benson was much happier this morning, big smiles and bright eyes, and a Hungry Hippo indeed. He ate all his cereal and Gideon was cleaning him up when Toby came in holding two cups of coffee.

He handed one to Gideon. "Thank you."

Toby sat on the sofa, sipped his coffee, and sighed. "So, about last night."

Oh boy.

This had been a yo-yo of a morning.

"Yeah, about last night," Gideon began.

"I just want to say," Toby added quickly, "that I have no regrets, at all. And I wouldn't object to more of the same. But . . ." he said, making a face. "I'm fairly sure you're about to say something responsible and reasonable, which I will totally understand."

Gideon shrugged. "I've tried to have the responsible and reasonable conversation with myself."

"Any luck?"

"None."

"Me either." Toby sighed, leaned back, and crossed his legs, and he smiled behind his coffee. "I'd be lying if I said I wasn't attracted to you. I mean, you're really hot."

Gideon almost spilled his coffee.

Toby smirked. "But I know work is work, and things only get complicated if we let them, right? We can set some ground rules."

"Benson has to be our priority," Gideon said. "That's my only stipulation."

"One hundred percent agree." Toby nodded. "If things get too weird, we cool it and go back to normal. We're both adults. We can do that, right?"

Gideon tried to swallow and failed, then he tried to sip his coffee and couldn't quite manage that either. He wasn't sure he'd be able to just cool it and pretend he didn't have feelings for him.

"So," Toby continued, "our days remain as they always have—you do your job, I'll do mine—but our nights can get a little more interesting. If you know what I mean."

Gideon smiled. "You've given this some thought."

"Not really. I've never had *interesting nights* with anyone I've worked for before, so I'm just trying to think of things I should say."

"Fair enough."

Toby studied Gideon for a few long seconds and he felt very scrutinised. "Are you sure you're okay with this, Gideon? Because you're not saying much."

His head was starting to spin.

"I'm very okay with this," he replied. "It's all very new and you're very forthright about such things. For what it's worth, I find you very attractive too." He tried not to blush. "I've tried to not think of you that way for a while now."

"Any luck?"

He chuckled. "None."

Toby smiled as he sipped his coffee and Gideon wasn't sure what to say next. They probably still had things to discuss, but he needed to get his head around everything first.

"Just so you know," Toby said, "I'm vers. Top or bottom, I'm bossy either way."

Gideon's coffee came out his nose.

TOBY WASN'T SURE WHY HE WAS BEING SO DEMANDING. Apart from the reason that he'd never wanted anyone so much in his life, and also aside from the fact that Gideon was being all shy and blushing, it was endearing.

And hot.

What they'd done last night was fuelled by pure desire. Sure, Toby had had sexual encounters that were hot before, but with Gideon there was an emotional need along with the physical.

He wanted Gideon.

Body and heart.

So he could get up the morning after and be all awkward and self-doubting, or he could get up and be a show of confidence and certainty. Toby had been told he was bossy his whole life, so why should this be any different?

He also knew that if Gideon detected a hint of doubt, he'd spiral into a what-have-I-done nosedive, coupled with the guilt of abusing his position of employee/power. Which was utterly ridiculous because it was Toby who was calling the shots.

Bossy, remember?

So he stated from the get-go that he wanted more of the same, laid down some quick ground rules that seemed appropriate, and let the chips fall where they may.

Gideon had gone to work with a smile and a hint of wonder in his eyes, and Toby knew he'd made the right call.

Gideon wanted him—Toby had no doubt of that. He just never would've acted on it without encouragement.

When Benson went down for a nap, Toby took out his

phone and called his brother. Josh answered on the fourth ring. "I'm at work, this better be good."

"I had sex with Gideon."

Josh made a strangled noise. "You what?"

"Well, not sex-sex, but sexual relations, if you know what I mean."

Then he shouty-whispered into the phone. "You what?!" It sounded like he was walking. Then a door opened, followed by the sounds of wind and traffic. He'd clearly gone outside. "Toby, we talked about this. You weren't going to do anything!"

"Well," Toby hedged. "You know what they say about the road to hell and good intentions."

"Tell me what happened?"

"You want details? Brother, I don't think—"

"Not those details, dick for brains. What happened after? Are you fired?"

"No." Toby scoffed incredulously. "We've agreed to expand our working relationship."

"Ah, jeez. You know this won't end well. How can this end well? How, Toby?"

"I don't know. We've just agreed to cool it if things get weird."

Josh snorted. "Weird, huh? By whose definition of weird is the yardstick here, Toby?"

Toby chuckled. "Yardstick. You've been hanging out with Pops too much. Are you eighty years old?"

Josh sighed. "This will end badly, and I'm trying to be the voice of reason."

"Well, in the event that it all goes to hell, you can say I told you so. But until then, you can chill."

"So I'm assuming it was good then. Everything you wanted, Mr Magnum PI is great in the sack, and—"

"He's Magnum, all right."

"Ah jeez, Tobes. No thanks."

"And Benson got his first two teeth, so it's been a very big day in this house."

Josh sighed again and it sounded as if he ran his hand over his face. "You wanna know what I think?"

"Not particularly."

"I think you're in over your head. I think you're playing house right now with the sexy single dad and his cute kid. I think you're not treating this as a job, but more of a relationship, and I don't know how that can possibly end well for you."

"Well, thanks for your input, Mr Optimistic."

"I don't wanna see you get hurt, Tobes," he said gently. "You already like this guy. You're already not thinking clearly because your heart is making decisions. And your dick, apparently."

Toby snorted. "Well, my heart and my dick outnumber my brain, so . . ."

"I can't talk you out of this, can I? There's no point in trying to reason with you."

"Nope. Just be there with the I-told-you-so chocolates when I'm broken hearted and unemployed."

Josh mumbled something and sighed again. "I will. Am I still picking you up on Friday?"

Oh. Friday. Toby hadn't thought about spending the weekend away from Gideon. He knew he should. He needed some time off work because he'd been sick last weekend and he'd not gone home to his parents' place.

But the idea of leaving Gideon and Benson made him sad.

"Yeah, I guess. Friday at six."

"Jesus Christ, you have it bad already. It's one weekend,

135

Toby. You need some time away from him," Josh said. "Maybe some time apart will help you see things a little clearly. Maybe Mum can talk some sense into you."

"It was Mum who put us in the same bed. She started this whole thing."

"She what? You know what? Never mind. She came home telling us all how wonderful Benson was and how adorable Gideon was."

Toby laughed. "Tell her I'll buy dinner on Friday night."

"As long as you don't cook it. I don't wanna die of food poisoning."

"You won't die. You'll wish for death, many times, although the chances of it actually killing you are slim."

"I gotta go back to work. Just try and keep your dick in your pants until you've talked to Mr Moustache about what happens to your job when this all goes to shit."

"I'll try."

Toby disconnected the call midway through Josh's sigh.

He knew every single thing Josh had said warranted some further thought, and it probably held more truth than Toby was willing to admit.

Was he playing house?

Hmm, the fact that Toby didn't want to answer that was the answer in itself. Was he pretending they were having some kind of relationship? That he was the stay-at-home partner of the successful and incredibly gorgeous dad?

Maybe.

Was it hurting anyone? Was it harmful to pretend such things? As long as he kept reality in check, Toby reasoned he'd be fine.

He wasn't in a relationship with Gideon. They had an arrangement. A night-time arrangement that didn't affect their daytime arrangements. He was Benson's nanny during the day, Gideon's lover at night.

It didn't have to be complicated.

Josh was just being a worrier, that was all.

Right?

Toby put it all aside while he did his morning chores, and when Benson woke up, they spent some time in the garden, then Toby read him some books, and then Benson had some floor time under his play gym.

All while Toby tried really hard not to think about what Josh had said.

When it was time to FaceTime Gideon for Benson's usual lunchtime video chat with his dadda, Toby sat with Benson on his lap, like he normally did, and held the phone out so it was only Benson's face he could see.

Only when Gideon answered, he could see he was in a café. "Say hello to Dadda," Toby said. Benson babbled away and tried to grab the phone, and Gideon's smiling face panned over to Lauren.

"Hello, Toby," she said with a hint of a stern smile.

"Lauren," Gideon said off-screen.

"Gideon has a really interesting mark on his neck."

Toby blinked. "Oh."

"Wouldn't happen to know anything about that?"

Oh my god.

Her stare. Her tone. Was this the best-friend shakedown?

"I do actually," Toby said. "Mosquitos were really bad here last night. It was quite a nasty bite and he kept scratching it. I told him not to."

She smirked. "Funny, that's not what he said."

"Oh?"

"Well, he didn't have to say anything, actually. I could

tell by the look on his face. And then I saw the mark under his collar. I mean, god, did you actually draw blood?"

Toby laughed. "Not that I remember."

Gideon snatched the phone back and rolled his eyes. "Sorry about that. I thought she might want to see Benson's two first teeth, not begin an interrogation."

Toby laughed. "It's fine. I just had a similar conversation with my brother, which was a lot of fun."

"Oh."

"Let's look at these teeth," Toby said, changing the subject. He held the phone so Benson's face was close and goosed his tummy to make him smile.

"Ooh, I saw them!" Lauren said.

Gideon's smile made Toby's belly tighten and his heart squeeze. Before he could say something foolish, he waved Benson's chubby little hand. "Say bye, Dadda. See you tonight."

Gideon's smile became something else. Serene, easy. And a little sad, maybe. "See you tonight."

"Steak and salad for dinner," Toby added before he ended the call. "I can't kill us with undercooked steak."

Gideon grinned. "Sounds good."

Toby ended the call with Gideon's happy face burned into his brain.

He didn't care about the consequences. He just wanted to see Gideon smile.

Chapter Twelve

TOBY WAS ON THE FLOOR WITH BENSON WHEN GIDEON got home. Not for any other reason than it was fun, and it was good sometimes to get on Benson's level. Dinner would take all of five minutes to cook, and the laundry was done, so lying on the blanket while some kid's TV shows played in the background wasn't a bad way to spend the evening.

Not to mention he'd not slept much the night before.

He was hoping for the same lack of sleep tonight too. He wasn't going to say no to more orgasms. He just hoped Gideon didn't have a change of heart while he was at work or that Lauren had managed to talk some sense into him.

Gideon's keys rattled in the door, and he stopped when he came inside and found them both on the floor. "Oh, everything okay?"

"We are having a great day," Toby said, looking up at him. "If you would like to take my place, I'll start dinner."

Gideon grinned. "Let me get changed first."

He came out wearing track shorts and an old tee shirt, looking much more comfortable. And happy, as he got down on the floor next to Benson.

"Oh, I see my handiwork is now a lovely shade of purple and red," Toby said, inspecting the hickey.

"Oh my god, it didn't help that Lauren poked and prodded it."

"Did anyone else say anything to you about it?"

He shook his head, and picking Benson up, he gave him a big raspberry kiss. "No."

"I'll be sure to leave them where no one can see them next time," Toby said.

Gideon's eyes cut to his, and he smirked. "You said you had a similar conversation with your brother?"

Toby sighed. "Oh yes. The one and only voice of reason."

"That good, huh?"

"He said I should be more worried about losing my job."

Gideon sat up. "What?"

"That if things go pear-shaped, you'd fire me?"

"I wouldn't."

"You could, though."

"Are you worried about that? Because I wouldn't do that to you. We agreed that Benson is our number one priority, and if things get skewed on that, then we take a step back."

"I'm not worried," Toby said with a shrug. "Benson will always be my number one priority. Not you, sorry. And not even me."

Gideon smiled. "Don't apologise."

"And complicated is just a state of mind," Toby added, not entirely believing that, but anyway. "Plus, my brother used the word yardstick in a sentence today, so everything he said is null and void."

Gideon was clearly confused for a second. "Is that a bad word?" He lay Benson back on the blanket and gave him his caterpillar to play with.

"It isn't a good word. He's not eighty years old. Why use yardstick when benchmark or measure was right there?"

"Right." Gideon's eyes were full of humour and spark. "Lauren's interrogation of me included no such words as yardstick or benchmark. Though she did use idiot a lot, while referring to me, not you. And she said I needed to include more iron in my diet because of the size of the hickey you gave me."

Toby inspected the hickey. "I'm not even remotely sorry about that."

Gideon snorted. "I told her I thought you were proud of it."

Toby preened a little. "I am. And speaking of iron, just as well we're having steak for dinner."

He got up and walked to the kitchen, happy and pleased that he and Gideon were able to talk about things—

"Toby!"

Gideon's panicked voice made Toby dash for the lounge room. "What?"

Gideon was still sitting on the floor, his eyes wide.

"He rolled over!"

Benson was now on his back.

"Oh my god!" Toby's shock gave way to excitement.

"He totally watched you walk out, followed you with his eyes, and rolled over."

"Two teeth and rolling over all in one day!"

Gideon looked a little dismayed. "He's growing up too fast. My little baby . . ." There was a sadness in his eyes. "I wish I could stop time."

He has no idea what he's in for, Toby thought. *Then again, what parent does?*

Toby went to Gideon and put his hand on his shoulder. "Don't be sad. Enjoy every stage, every milestone, every minute of this. He'll be a screaming tantrum-throwing toddler soon enough."

Gideon smiled at him in such a way that Toby almost leaned down and kissed him. He had to physically stop himself, but not before he looked at Gideon's lips and back into his eyes.

But his lips . . .

Dinner, Toby.

Right.

Their arrangement was for nights only, right?

Toby pulled his hand away and had to take a breath. "I should make dinner."

AFTER BENSON'S BATH AND BED ROUTINE, GIDEON SAT on the sofa next to Toby, with his foot tucked up under his arse and a cup of tea in both hands. He chewed on his bottom lip, and although he was staring at the TV, Toby was sure he wasn't paying any attention to it.

"Trying to say something?" Toby asked.

Gideon shot him a look and laughed. "Am I that obvious?"

"You're nervous."

Gideon studied him for a long moment. "You can read me so well. Something Drew never bothered with, I realise now."

"He didn't bother with a lot of things, by the sounds of it."

"No, he didn't."

"Do you miss him?"

Gideon seemed surprised by this question. "No. Not at all. In the beginning, maybe. I can't even say I missed the help because he never helped with anything. Not with Benson, not with me." He shrugged. "I missed what I thought we had, the perfect idea of us I had conjured up in my head, which I can see now was nothing even close to perfect. It was the opposite of perfect."

"I'd have never thought it was possible to dislike someone I've never met. What he did to you was a really shitty thing to do. And if karma were to give him an unscratchable itch for the rest of his life, I wouldn't be mad."

Gideon chuckled. "Me either." Then he sighed. "I never thought in a million years I'd be a single parent. Drew and I had been together for years. I thought we were solid. Then my sister called and told me she was pregnant, that she was giving the baby up for adoption. I was shocked, it was all so out of the blue. Maybe in hindsight I can see I didn't really give Drew an option. But this baby was my blood. Adopting him was the right thing to do, and I was doing it with or without Drew." Gideon shrugged. "Thank god only *I* adopted him. Thank god Drew said no to being his adoptive parent. I mean, it was easier with just me because I was a blood relative, and my sister was happy with that. Drew wanted nothing to do with any of it. Not the adoption, not Benson."

"Which turned out to be a good thing," Toby added. "I know it must have been awful and difficult in the beginning. But if he wasn't one hundred percent on board with Benson, then you and Benson are better off without him."

Gideon nodded. "True. Could you imagine if he was on the adoption papers as a father?" Gideon shuddered.

Yeah, thank god, indeed.

Toby was glad he didn't have to deal with Drew. The

idea of anyone hurting Gideon and resenting Benson . . . It made Toby angry. He needed to change the subject.

What were we talking about? Oh yeah . . .

"So what did you want to talk about? What were you chewing on your bottom lip about before?"

"Oh." He worried his bottom lip again. "God, this is embarrassing, so I'm just going to say it. I'm vers too. This morning you just blurted it out like you were discussing the weather."

"And your coffee came out of your nose."

"It cleared the sinuses, that was for sure."

Toby laughed. "And it was totally sexy. Very becoming."

"Oh, good."

"So you're versatile too, huh?"

Gideon let out a nervous breath and put his tea down, probably before it came out his nose like his coffee had. "Yes. I've always liked both aspects of sex. I mean, I like all aspects of sex. But I like to be able to give whatever my partner wants. It just depends on the mood or whatever." He ran his hand through his hair and kept talking a bit too fast. "I've never actually had any kind of ongoing sexual relationship with another vers guy. I've only ever been with guys who preferred one or the other, or no anal sex at all, or whatever. Everyone's different, which I can appreciate. That's totally fine."

Toby reached over and gave Gideon's hand a squeeze. "You wanna take a breath for me?"

Gideon barked out a laugh. "I don't know why I'm so nervous." He inhaled deeply and let it out slowly. "I guess what I'm trying to say is that I don't know, with two vers guys, how we navigate it."

"Like toss a coin or write up a roster?" Gideon stared at him, and it made Toby laugh. "I'm kidding! Gideon, we just take it easy. Don't stress about it. If you need a good dicking to relieve some stress, then that's what we do. Or if I need to get pounded into the mattress, we do that instead."

Gideon's eyes were now comically wide, and Toby was glad he wasn't holding a hot tea.

"Did you not talk about what you wanted with your ex?" Toby asked.

"No. We just assumed our roles, him as the top and me as the bottom, and that's what we did." His cheeks were a deep red.

"Well, we're going to be grown-ups and talk about these things," Toby said. "Like tonight, I think it's too soon for any dicking, but I'm all for some sucking and cuddling afterwards."

Gideon covered his face with his hands and fell against the back of the sofa. "Oh my god." When he lowered his hands, he was smiling. "How do you just say this stuff?"

Toby laughed and set his cup of tea down. He crept over and straddled Gideon's lap. Gideon was clearly surprised, but his hands found Toby's hips. Toby lifted Gideon's chin, forcing his head back, and he gave him an almost-kiss.

"I will always say what needs saying. I'm bossy, remember?"

Gideon's eyes went to Toby's lips and drew slowly back up to his eyes. "Bossy works for me."

Toby began to rock a little, their bodies touching in all the right places. "I want to take you to bed," he said. "And I want to taste you. If that's okay with you?"

Gideon's nostrils flared and he rolled his hips up to meet Toby. "That's very okay with me. Can I taste you too?"

Toby lightly touched his index finger to Gideon's bottom lip. "I will insist you do."

The smirk Gideon gave him was sublime. Holding Gideon's chin, Toby kissed him, opening his lips with his own and sinking his tongue into his mouth.

Gideon groaned and the hold on Toby's hips tightened.

He was such a good kisser. Toby could kiss him forever, and straddling him and gyrating like this, Toby wondered if he could come without touching his dick.

He probably could.

But he wanted something else tonight.

Breaking the kiss, Toby peeled himself off Gideon and stood up. He held out his hand, which Gideon took, and he led him to Gideon's room. It was dark, a crack of light from the open door the only illumination.

Toby pulled his shirt off and stood there, letting Gideon's eyes rake over him. Having a man look at him with pure lust was a powerful drug. His skin prickled, flushed warm, and he undid his pants and let them fall down, standing there in only his briefs.

Gideon stared at Toby's erection and Toby smiled as he gave himself a sensual pull. "You're way overdressed," Toby murmured.

Gideon pulled his shirt over his head and tossed it to the floor, slid his shorts and briefs down over his hips, and let his cock spring free.

Damn.

Toby went to him, taking Gideon's balls in his hand and crashing his mouth to his. He tugged and teased and sucked on his bottom lip, and Gideon shuddered. Toby broke the kiss, gave Gideon's cock a quick pump. "Sit on the edge of the bed."

Gideon sat and Toby went to his knees. He wasted no time in taking Gideon's cock into his mouth, tasting him, sucking and sliding up and down the shaft. Gideon cried out, his hand fisting Toby's hair.

Toby smiled around his cockhead, loving how Gideon was losing control.

His erection was thick and hot, and Toby could only imagine how it would feel inside him. The very idea of it made him groan.

Gideon flexed his hips and Toby took him in deeper, sliding his hand up and down the base, pumping him.

"Oh god, Toby," Gideon bit out. His cock was now impossibly hard, swollen, and Toby knew he was close.

So he sucked harder, pumped him, and took him into his throat.

Gideon's hold of Toby's hair tightened, and he trembled with restraint as his cock throbbed and spilled into Toby's throat.

Fuck yes.

Before Gideon could come back to reality, Toby stood up, pulled his cock out of his briefs, and tapped Gideon's bottom lip with it.

He opened his mouth, his eyes dreamy, and Toby slipped his cock inside. Gideon flattened his tongue and pulled Toby all the way in, taking him straight into his throat, and swallowed around him.

"Fucking hell," Toby yelped, unprepared for the total onslaught of pleasure, but Gideon held his arse, keeping him right there.

Buried.

Toby could feel himself twitching, swelling, and Gideon swallowed again, breathing through his nose, and he groaned. The sound vibrated through Toby's cock, and when Gideon touched Toby's balls, slipping a finger in behind them, Toby came without warning.

"Fuck, oh god, yes," he hissed as he shot his load down Gideon's throat.

It hit him so hard and fast his head spun, and his bones turned to jelly. Gideon pulled off and helped Toby lie down, his body still twitching as Gideon wrapped his arms around him.

"You okay in there?"

"Nnn," Toby managed to say. It took a second for his brain to come back online. "Can't speak."

Gideon laughed, rubbing Toby's back.

"Where did you learn how to do that?"

"Dick sucking school."

"Hmm. Please tell me you were the teacher's pet and he gave you private lessons for being such a good boy."

Gideon laughed really loudly. "Ah no. But I think I've seen that porno."

Toby chuckled. "Same."

They were quiet then, simply holding each other, tracing patterns on skin until they both fell asleep.

Toby expected Josh's car to turn up on Friday night at six but it didn't.

It was his mum.

Carla came down the path, smiling brightly, carrying a foiled tray of something.

"Oh god," Toby whispered. "I apologise now for anything she says that may embarrass you. Or me."

Gideon laughed and opened the door. "Carla, please come in."

"Oh, thank you, dear," she said. "And don't you look so much better than the last time I saw you?"

"Well, I'm no longer green, so there's that."

"Mum," Toby said with a questioning, warning tone. "What are you doing here?"

"Josh had to work late, and I brought this." She lifted the foil-covered tray. "I thought Gideon might be here by himself all weekend, so I made him some of Nonna's special recipe lasagne."

"With her homemade passata?"

"Of course," she replied. Then she shoved the tray in Toby's general direction. "Take this. Where is that gorgeous little jelly bean?" She looked around the room, found Benson under his play gym, and went over to him.

Toby wasn't sure what to say or do. He just shrugged, holding the lasagne. "This has my nonna's homemade passata."

Gideon was grinning now. "I'm sure it'll be amazing."

"I don't think you understand," Toby hissed at him. "This means you've basically been adopted, brought into the brood, worthy enough to consume the family's sacred holy grail. My nonna makes the sauce, my nonno bottles it. It's a whole thing."

"Oh," he replied, still amused. "I'm honoured."

"When did this little sausage get two teeth?" Carla asked. She now had Benson on her knee, bouncing him gently.

"Just yesterday, Mum."

She only then seemed to realise Toby was still holding the tray of lasagne. "Hurry up and put that in the kitchen, Toby. I need to get home for dinner. Your great aunt Mary's waiting, and I've got food in the oven."

Toby rolled his eyes, wishing even more now that he could stay with Gideon and Benson.

Gideon was trying not to smile.

He gave the tray to him to hold. "Is there another lasagne for us at home?"

"No." Carla put Benson in his bouncer, and she stood up. "We're having chicken."

Toby grimaced. "Not chicken. Anything but chicken."

Carla ushered him out the door so fast he barely had time to collect his bag. He managed to mouth 'can I please stay with you?' while his mum reminded him she'd never given anyone food poisoning yet.

Gideon's beautiful smiling face was the last thing Toby saw before the door closed.

Chapter Thirteen

GIDEON MUST HAVE SMILED FOR A FULL HOUR AFTER Toby and his mum left. He missed having a parent that cared, that fussed over him and made sure he'd eaten.

And the lasagne?

To die for.

He couldn't resist sending Toby a photo of his scraped-clean plate with a quick text.

> Delicious. Best lasagne I've ever had.
> Please give my compliments to the chef.

Toby's reply came through a few moments later.

> I hate you so much right now. I had chicken marsala. Still good but my stomach is no longer a fan of chicken. Please save some lasagne for me. I'll be so grateful.

Gideon smiled at his phone. There was enough lasagne to feed a family of six. There was no way he could eat it all in two days, but he couldn't resist playing along a little.

I'll think about it.

Toby didn't reply for a while, so Gideon settled into his evening. Benson was fed and sound asleep in bed, and Gideon had a cup of raspberry tea while he watched a travel show about hiking in Peru.

It wasn't the same without Toby.

He would have commented on the food and the remarkable scenery, the culture. He also would have taken the piss out of the fashion choices of the two hikers, and Gideon couldn't help but wonder how Toby was spending his night.

Was he missing Gideon at all?

Like he could read Gideon's mind, Gideon's phone buzzed. It was a photo of a table with playing cards, the hands of six people visible, some small drinking glasses with what looked like sherry or port.

I'm playing Euchre with a bunch of old Italians like I'm in the Godfather. Send help.

Gideon smiled.

Are you winning?

Are you kidding? No one can beat my grandpa. He's been playing this since he was eight. I know this because he tells me every time we play.

Gideon laughed, but it made something ache inside him. He longed for what Toby had. He longed for that family connection, to be playing cards with his parents and grandparents.

Wish I was there.

> Can you play Euchre?

> Nope.

> Well at least then there'd be someone worse than me.

Gideon snorted, but he wasn't sure what to say. He wanted to chat all night. He wanted to call him, to hear his voice. Which was ridiculous. Toby needed to spend this time with his family. He needed time off work.

Realising he and Benson were work to Toby made Gideon feel uneasy.

And sad.

> Enjoy your night.

> What are you doing tonight?

> Watching Travelling Idiots Do Peru. You'd be horrified at the hiking footwear choices.

He replied with two laughing faces.
Gideon smiled at his phone for a long while.

> Goodnight, Toby.

> Night xx

When Gideon climbed into bed, he stared at the ceiling for far too long. He wished Toby was in bed with him, curled around him, holding him. He wished he could kiss him and touch his face, and he wished they could fall asleep in each other's arms.

Instead, loneliness settled in beside him, and reality

plagued his dreams. He finally had with Toby what he thought he wanted. He'd told himself it was enough.

But now it wasn't.

He wanted more.

SUNDAY COULDN'T GET HERE QUICK ENOUGH FOR Gideon. He'd spent the morning with Lauren and Jill, helping them plan their holiday. Or, mostly, he was insanely jealous as they organised hotels and snorkelling in Fiji while bouncing Benson on his knee, pretending he wasn't pining hopelessly for Toby.

Because missing someone like that after only two days was kinda pathetic.

"And how's the new arrangement going with Toby?" Lauren asked.

Jill smirked, nudging him. "Lauren told me."

"I figured she would."

"The hickey would have been a giveaway," she replied. She inspected his neck. "Which is now a faded yellowish colour. Very nice."

Gideon sighed. "The arrangement is going fine. Great, actually. He's great."

Lauren stared at him. "Gideon."

She'd always been able to see through him. "It's been two days," he blurted out. "Two days. That's all. And I miss him. Which is stupid and not part of our arrangement. I don't know what I'm doing. I'm older than him, I should have more self-control. But he's all cool, calm, and collected, and I'm a hot fucking mess."

"How do you know he's not at his parents' house being a hot fucking mess?" Jill asked.

"Because he's out doing stuff. He was going to the markets this morning with his mum and then to the beach with his brother this afternoon."

Lauren's brows knitted. "How do you know this? You're not stalking him on his socials, are you?"

"What? No!" Gideon cried. "We text each other."

They both stared at him again. "That's a very boyfriend-ish agreement you have going on there," Jill said. Before Gideon could object, she put her hands up. "I'm not saying it's a bad thing. In fact, I think it's great."

Boyfriend-ish?

Ah, jeez. Gideon's head swam.

"But?" he asked.

"But it's happened so soon," Jill said suddenly.

Lauren shook her head. "No, it's not. Remember, I was dating Thea when I met you."

"But that was different."

"No it wasn't. We just knew from the second we met," Lauren said with a shrug. "And I'm thinking Gideon here knew the second he met Toby that he was going to be someone important in his life." She took a deep breath and sighed with a smile. "At first I thought you were all caught up in it, Gideon, and that it was a rebound thing. But now I'm thinking it could be the real thing."

"The real thing?"

"You really like him, don't you?" she pressed. "You miss him, you think about him all the time. You get all jittery at the thought of him, and we can all see the stupid look you get on your face."

"It's not stupid."

She imitated a person who'd smoked too much weed. "You get that dreamy look in your eyes and a dopey smile."

Gideon smiled and then he laughed. "Okay, okay. I do

really like him. Which is the stupid part. Because there's no way he can feel the same. And we still have the whole boss-slash-employee issue."

"You're having sex with him," Jill said. "That horse has already bolted and now you want to try and shut the gate?"

"Well, no . . . I don't want to shut that gate. I want to leave it wide open."

Lauren patted Gideon's knee. "I'm happy for you, Gideon. I'm happy that you're happy and that you've found someone who treats you right. He looks after you, he cares about Benson." She wiggled his little foot. "And he's vers. He's kinda perfect for you."

Jill gasped. "He is? You never told me that." She aimed a pointed glare at Lauren. "That's like finding a jigsaw piece that fits on all the sides."

Gideon laughed off his embarrassment. "Uh, thanks. I think."

Lauren sighed. "I still think you and he need to have a little chat. I would say before your heart gets involved, but I think it's too late for that."

Gideon groaned. "I don't want to ruin it. Can't I just enjoy it before reality rains all over me?"

Jill made a face. "I say enjoy it. You're already in with both feet, so you've got nothing to lose. Maybe lure him into the water a little."

Lauren gasped out a laugh. "You can't do that!"

"Yes, he can."

"If you don't want to ask him outright, how about you just read his reactions," Lauren tried. "See what he does when he gets home. See if he missed you as much as you missed him."

"Like what?"

"Well, if he comes in and goes to his room or plants

himself on the couch, glued to his phone, then maybe he's not as excited as you might want him to be."

Gideon could do that. He didn't want to just ask him outright if he was into this arrangement as much as Gideon was. It would just make things awkward, and Gideon didn't want to risk Toby saying no and losing what they had. Or worse, Toby walking out of their lives for good . . .

Lauren gave him a gentle shake. "Stop overthinking it," she said. "I can see your mind ticking over and going into every possible scenario already. Just take it a day at a time, Gideon. And see what he does when he gets home."

He nodded lamely. "Okay."

And just before six o'clock, Gideon's nerves were in tatters. His stomach was a ball of knotted grease, and it was ridiculous that he should get himself so worked up. He was in the kitchen with an unhappy Benson on his hip, because of course Benson decided he needed food right then. Gideon was mixing the Farex cereal to the right consistency and Benson was trying to help when the sound of keys jiggled in the front door, followed by a very familiar, "Hey."

"In the kitchen," Gideon called out. "Benson, you can't have it yet."

Toby appeared, smiling fondly. He walked in, put a tray of something on the table, then wrapped his arms around both of them, first giving Gideon a kiss on the cheek, then Benson.

A kiss? During the day? When their 'arrangement' had been for after-hours only. Surely that had to mean something, right?

Toby kept his hand on Gideon's back. "Miss me?"

If only he knew.

He was going to joke. He was going to aim for funny,

but in that moment, he decided to go with the truth. He looked Toby right in the eye when he replied. "Yes."

"Of course you missed me," Toby said, taking Benson out of Gideon's arms. "And did this little chicky nuggy grow while I was away? I'm sure he's bigger."

"It might explain the appetite," Gideon said, finally getting the Farex mixed properly. "We're trying the new one with apple in it."

"Ooh." Toby got Benson all situated in his bouncer with a bib and they sat next to each other on the sofa while Gideon fed Benson spoonful after spoonful like he was a starving baby bird.

"I think he likes it," Toby said with a laugh.

"He's been a hungry boy all day."

Toby found himself leaning against Gideon, probably more than was necessary, but he didn't care.

He'd had a very thought-provoking weekend. Well, it wasn't so much thought-provoking as it was his mother asking about the marks on Gideon's neck. That was ten seconds into their car ride on Friday night. And then, of course, Josh had thrown him under the bus when he'd asked, in front of everyone, how his new boss was in bed.

Yep.

In front of everyone.

His entire family always had a very honest relationship, and even with his being gay, no one ever cared. His nonna asked about his boyfriends like she asked Josh about his girl-friends. It was just how it was.

When they'd asked if he was in that kind of relationship

with his boss, he'd replied with a very honest, "It's not like that."

"But do you want it to be?" his mother asked. "He's a very nice man. Very handsome. Gorgeous son. Nice house."

Toby knew there was no way he was getting out of the conversation, like he knew he couldn't deny it or lie to them. Because Toby did want that kind of relationship with Gideon.

"It's complicated," he'd said. "And nothing for anyone to worry about."

Which of course made them all worry even more. And Toby knew it was only because his parents cared, but he'd lost track of how many times his mum asked him what he wanted with Gideon and to make sure he answered from his heart.

It was his heart that scared him the most.

"My mum gave me some leftovers," Toby said, rubbing Gideon's back as he fed Benson. "She insisted I bring them, and if you know my mother, it's really in everyone's best interest not to argue."

"Are you kidding?" Gideon asked. "I would never argue. That lasagne was the best thing I've ever eaten."

"Did you save me some?"

"Of course."

Toby kissed Gideon's shoulder, and Benson yelled at Gideon for not feeding him fast enough.

"Okay, okay. Seems someone found his temper."

Toby laughed and, still rubbing Gideon's back, smiled at Benson. "I missed you guys."

Gideon froze for a second, then looked at him, his eyes full of fire and honesty. He leaned in, capturing Toby's lips in a soft kiss. Warm, serene. Perfect.

Until Benson yelled at him again.

Gideon jumped, then chuckled, embarrassed. "Okay, okay, jeez, Mister Impatient, who can't possibly be starving after all he's eaten today."

When the bowl was scraped clean, Gideon gave Benson the soft rubber spoon. He clenched it in his little fist, his babbles and non-stop gibberish happier now.

Toby *had* missed them.

Both of them.

Sure, when he'd worked with other families, he'd always enjoyed seeing them again after time away. But he'd never missed them, and certainly not after just two days.

Being back with them now felt so right.

They had a busy hour or so, with their dinner and giving Benson a bath and bottle. Toby stood by the door in the hall and listened as Gideon sang his bedtime song and read him a story, his voice low and soothing. It put Benson to sleep but it did the opposite to Toby.

It made his heart swell, and it made him ache with emotions he wasn't ready to name.

When Gideon stepped out and quietly closed the door, he was clearly surprised to see Toby in the hall, leaning against the wall. "Oh, hey."

Smiling, Toby took his hand. "That song you sing to him is the sweetest thing." He pulled him closer, their bodies flush. He held Gideon's face, running his thumb along his scruffy jaw. "I've missed your moustache."

Gideon sputtered out a laugh. "You missed what?"

Toby's thumb flattened the edge of Gideon's moustache. "Kissing you, and the feel of your moustache," Toby murmured. "I really like it."

Gideon ran his hand down Toby's side and over his arse. "Did you want a cup of tea tonight?"

"Absolutely not."

Gideon walked Toby backward into his room. "Thank god," he mumbled before capturing Toby's mouth with his own. They stood there beside the bed, kissing, tasting, and reacquainting with wandering hands and lazy tongues.

Toby was in no hurry to get to the finish line tonight. He wanted to savour it, enjoy it. And Gideon wasn't in a rush either. The way he held Toby's face, gentle and sweet, how his fingers danced over his skin down his neck, and how he sighed and moaned like he found it all so . . . exquisite.

No, there was no rush at all.

And hours later, when they finally did fall asleep, they were wound around each other so tight, Toby wasn't sure where he ended and Gideon began.

He wasn't sure he wanted to know.

MONDAY NIGHT WAS THE SAME. GIDEON GOT HOME from work, greeted them both with the biggest grin and gave them both a kiss.

And Tuesday, and Wednesday, and Thursday.

Small touches, gentle and brief kisses, warm private smiles during the day. And long make-out sessions and unhurried orgasms at night.

It was beginning to feel a lot like lovemaking.

Toby wanted to have sex with him. They'd done almost everything but have penetrative sex. They'd come close. They'd teased and taunted, brushing his cock against Gideon's hole, and Gideon doing the same. It was going to happen, and once Toby had decided he wanted it, he made sure Gideon knew.

He'd disappeared into his bathroom while Gideon

bathed Benson, and by the time he'd put him to bed, he was ready.

Gideon was sitting on the sofa when Toby walked out. "I've just put the kettle on," he said. Then he studied Toby's face as he walked toward him. "Are you feeling okay? You were gone a while."

Toby slid one knee onto the sofa and straddled Gideon's hips, slowly lowering himself down. "I feel great," Toby murmured. "I was just taking care of myself. Getting myself ready." Toby tipped Gideon's chin up, forcing his head back with a bruising kiss. "I want you inside me tonight."

Gideon let out a shuddering breath, lips wet and pupils blown, his hands gripping Toby's hips. "Toby," he breathed, whispering his name like a prayer.

And for a brief, horrible moment, Toby thought Gideon might say no.

But then Gideon reached up, gripped Toby's jaw, his thumb sliding into his mouth, and he drove his hips up as Toby brought his face down for another kiss. It was messy and desperate, and so fucking hot.

Toby moaned, widening his knees, trying to grind down on Gideon.

Gideon broke the kiss to say just one word. "Bed."

Toby didn't need telling twice. He jumped up and pulled Gideon to his feet, almost dragging him into Gideon's room. Gideon stopped when he saw the condom and lube on his bed. His eyes shot to Toby's. "Presumptuous?"

Toby pulled his shirt off. "No. Confident." Then his boxer shorts. "And I'm horny and desperate, so get undressed."

Gideon's eyes widened and he laughed. "Oh. I forget how bossy you can be."

He still wasn't undressing fast enough, so Toby decided to help him. First his T-shirt, then his sweat shorts. His gorgeous cock was thick and heavy, and desire bloomed in Toby's belly. He gave Gideon a long, slow pull. "I want you so bad," he murmured, kissing the top of Gideon's shoulder as he stroked him.

Gideon pulled Toby's face up for a rough kiss, his moustache tickling. God, Toby loved it.

But he was desperate. And he was done waiting.

He broke the kiss and knelt in the middle of the bed. He made a show of stroking himself for Gideon. Then, ever so slowly, he bent down so he was on all fours, his back arched, his arse in the air. He reached down and pulled on his balls, giving himself another long, slow pull.

"Christ," Gideon breathed.

Without warning, Gideon's hands were on Toby's arse cheeks, spreading him wide, and a warm, wet tongue licked over Toby's hole.

Toby gripped the bedding. "Oh fuck."

Gideon worked his tongue inside him, sliding in and out, making Toby moan. Toby buried his face into the bed covers, fisting the fabric as he arched his back more.

Gideon fucked his hole with his tongue for an unbearable amount of time, then replaced his tongue with a finger, adding lube, then another finger. Stretching him, preparing him in the best of ways.

But it wasn't quite enough.

He was wanton, desperate for more, and not above begging. "Please, Gideon. Please hurry."

When he heard the rip of the foil, Toby smiled and sighed, relaxing his whole body. He was about to get what he wanted, what he needed. "Hell yes. Give it to me."

Gideon pressed his cock against Toby's hole, and Toby

held his breath. He pushed in, slow and big, breaching him so perfectly. Toby's eyes rolled back and his breath caught in his throat as Gideon slid inside him.

"Oh fuck, Toby," Gideon bit out. "You feel so good."

Toby had trouble catching his breath. Gideon was too big, too much, and—

"Breathe," Gideon murmured. He leaned down over Toby's back and kissed his spine. "Breathe."

Toby exhaled slowly and inhaled, relaxing his shoulders as he did. Gideon kissed his shoulder blade, his spine, licking and nipping the skin as his fingers dug into his hips, his cock pushing into the hilt.

Then he leaned back and changed the angle.

"Oh, holy fuck," Toby cried.

Gideon slid out and back in, again and again, slower at first, letting Toby adjust. Then faster and deeper, and Toby could only groan and mumble nonsensical things.

He was lost to it all.

Gideon owned his whole body.

"God, you feel so good," Gideon grunted as he fucked him. "You take it so well."

Then, gripping Toby's shoulder, he pulled him up onto his knees and slid his arm around Toby's chest, holding him against him, fucking him like that.

Toby's head fell back onto Gideon's shoulder. He felt split open and so very full; Gideon was balls deep inside him like this.

And when Gideon's hand wrapped around Toby's cock, he cried out, almost sobbing. He was so close, yet so impossibly far. Gideon had Toby on the brink.

"Need you to come," Gideon said, his voice rough in Toby's ear.

As if Toby's body obeyed Gideon's command, his balls

drew up, orgasm coiled tight, and with a few more strokes, he tumbled over the edge. Gideon held his hips, thrusting up as Toby came, sending his orgasm into the heavens.

Toby arched, strung tight, and cried out as he shot his load onto the towel. He collapsed onto Gideon, utterly boneless.

Gideon wasn't done. He pushed Toby's shoulder down to the mattress, hitched Toby's arse up, and plowed into him. Relentless and deep, he fucked him, and Toby took it all. He loved it. He wanted this forever. To be owned so completely, just like this.

He was Gideon's.

And then Gideon slammed into him one more time, fingers digging into Toby's hips, and he shuddered. His cock surged and twitched, filling the condom inside him with a loud groan.

Toby smiled into the mattress.

"Fuck yes."

Gideon collapsed on top of him, not moving except for ragged breaths and soft kisses on the nape of Toby's neck.

"You okay?" he murmured, his voice rough.

Toby chuckled. "I've never been better."

Toby could feel Gideon smile against his shoulder, followed by a soft kiss. He pulled out slowly and was gone, though Toby still couldn't move. Gideon came back with a wet washcloth and took care of him.

He collected Toby into his arms, and Toby slept like the dead.

Chapter Fourteen

GIDEON WAS UP BEFORE TOBY, WHICH WAS RARE. BUT considering what he'd done to him last night, Gideon wasn't surprised. He had Benson up and had given him a bottle before Toby stumbled out of bed.

"Good morning," Gideon said. "How'd you sleep?"

"Like I got railed into the mattress. How about you?"

Gideon sputtered. "Oh, well . . . Uh, yes, I slept very well, thank you."

"Oh, now you're all shy. You weren't shy last night." Toby smirked at him. "Sorry I didn't hear Benson. Has he been up long?"

Gideon shook his head. "No, it's fine. He's had a bottle. No doubt he'll want some Farex soon."

Toby nodded and then grimaced and rubbed his arse. "I don't think I'll be sitting down much today."

Gideon smiled . . . until he clued in what Toby meant. He was quickly horrified. "Oh my god, are you okay?"

Toby chuckled. "I'm so good. Still on cloud nine. Want some coffee?"

Gideon followed him into the kitchen. "Can I get you

166

anything? Are you sure you're okay?"

Toby flicked the kettle on and got two cups out of the cupboard. He turned to face Gideon. "Believe me when I say I am good. So good. Like, soooo good. I feel thoroughly had, and honestly, I can't wait for you to do it again."

Gideon wasn't sure about that, but he decided to take Toby at his word. "Let me make some toast."

They stood side by side in the kitchen, Toby making coffee, Gideon at the toaster. Toby bumped his hip to Gideon's. "And how are you feeling this morning?"

"Oh." Gideon's cheeks heated and he couldn't stop smiling. "I feel . . . great."

"You should too," Toby agreed. "You were great last night. Like, holy shit."

Gideon kept his gaze strictly on the toaster and chewed on his bottom lip. "So, uh . . . when do you think maybe you could—"

The toast popped and Gideon jumped.

Toby laughed. "You want me to do to you what you did to me?"

Gideon was too busy buttering the toast to look at him. "Well, maybe yes, that's what I was thinking."

Toby hummed. "It can't be tonight, because it's Friday and I have some stupid family dinner thing on this week-end, so my mum will be here at six on the dot because I have to help her with that." He rolled his eyes. "What about Sunday? I'll be back at six, Benson will be fed and asleep by seven, seven thirty. I can have you face down on the bed by eight."

Gideon stared at him. He swallowed hard. "Uhhh."

Toby smiled. He poured the boiling water into their cups, stirred, and handed one to Gideon. "I take it that's a yes."

Gideon's brain took a few seconds to catch up. "How am I supposed to work today thinking about that? Actually, now I'm going to be thinking about that all weekend."

"Good." He sipped his coffee and stole a piece of the buttered toast. "Thanks."

And of course, that was all Gideon thought about all day at work. Well, what Toby was going to do to him, and what he did to Toby last night. He'd never had sex like that with anyone before.

Never that intense. Never that emotionally charged.

He'd never needed to be that deep inside someone before. He wanted to crawl inside Toby. He wanted to never leave.

It was so much more than just sex.

He was busy at work, trying to get as much done as he could without his mind wandering to X-rated places every few minutes. Without thinking about Toby, and wishing he was at home with both his favourite boys.

Your favourite boys, Gideon? Really?

Just then, his phone chimed with a FaceTime. He hadn't realised the time . . .

Benson's beautiful face filled the screen. "Say hello to Dadda," Toby said off-screen.

"How's my beautiful boy?"

"He has hollow legs again today. Hungry and growing by the minute."

That made Gideon smile. "And how's . . ." *my other beautiful boy . . .* ? Gideon caught himself. "How's Toby this afternoon?"

The phone panned up to Toby's face. "Well, I'm sitting down," he said with a sly smile. "And I have bruises on my hips that look suspiciously like finger marks. Know anything about that?"

Gideon's eyes went wide. Thank god he was alone in his office. "Uhhh." He cleared his throat. "I'm so sorry. God, Toby. I didn't mean—"

"Don't apologise," he said sternly. He brought the phone in closer, giving him the stink eye. "Because you will be doing it again. Okay?"

Well. Right, then.

Heat bloomed in Gideon's chest. "I don't know what I prefer: Mr Bossy, or Mr Begging."

Toby's shocked face became a smirk. "Begging, huh?"

Gideon laughed. This was not a conversation suitable for work. "Okay, well, I should let you go."

"Uh, before you go, just real quick. And you can absolutely say no. In fact, I already said no on your behalf, but my mother will mention it, so I have to ask. She asked if you'd like to come to lunch tomorrow. It's a whole family thing. There will be second and third cousins and enough food to feed an army, and I know it's super random, and you absolutely don't have to answer because it's embarrassing enough. I think my mother's convinced you don't eat when I'm not here, and anyway, she insisted that I ask, even though I told her you don't need her fussing. So anyway, I'm sorry if it's awkward, but I know damn well she will bring it up when she picks me up tonight so I have to prewarn you—"

"Lunch? With your whole family?"

"All of us. And I do mean all of us. It's my aunt and uncle's forty-fifth wedding anniversary. It's my dad's eldest sister and she's like a second nonna—"

"I'd like to go."

The words were out before Gideon really knew what he was saying yes to. He knew it was a lunch with Toby's family, yes. But the ramifications . . . the implications . . .

They weren't dating. They weren't boyfriends. His entire extended family were about to assume they were, and maybe that was a bad idea . . .

But Gideon missed having a family.

"I mean, if it's okay with you," he added. "I don't mind. If you think it's weird, that's okay. But if your mum is gonna hassle you about me going, I'll just go. It's not like I have any other plans."

There was a beat of silence and Toby's face was so still and stunned, Gideon thought the phone might have frozen. "Oh. Uh, sure. I don't have a problem with it. I just assumed you wouldn't want to go. Do you know how many old Italian people you are about to meet? There will be questions and very little regard to embarrassment or discretion."

Gideon chuckled. "How bad could it be?"

The screen zoomed in on Toby's eyes. "What part of anything I've just said didn't you understand? On a scale of one to mortifying, it's a solid twelve. And you can forget seeing Benson for three hours. He'll be spoiled rotten by everyone and have his cheeks pinched a thousand times, and his first words will be 'bellisimo bambino'."

That made Gideon laugh. "Okay. I better go. I have work to do."

Toby put the screen on Benson. "Say bye to Dadda."

Benson's bright eyes and drooly smile filled the screen before the call ended, and Gideon sighed happily.

Was he about to meet Toby's entire family? Yes, he was. And be introduced as what, exactly? Toby's boss? Toby's friend? The dad of the baby that Toby nannied?

He wasn't sure, but he was excited about going.

"Do you know what you've done?" Toby asked pretty much as soon as Gideon walked through the door. "I told my mother, so that conversation was a lot of fun."

Gideon picked Benson up and gave him a big smoochy kiss. "You're welcome."

Toby rolled his eyes. "She wanted to know if she needed to buy a port-a-cot for her little jelly bean, just so you know. And if you liked acciughe al verde. I said you didn't, so you're welcome for that by the way."

Gideon wasn't sure what that was. But he mentioned a cot? "A port-a-cot? I hope you told her no."

"I told her no, of course. I mean, my god. And I also told her you were allergic to tomatoes and garlic and gluten."

Gideon stared. "Why would you say that?"

"So maybe next time she'd think twice before inviting you."

Gideon laughed. "Uh, thanks? She knows I ate the lasagne, right? She knows I'm not allergic to those things." Those three things were the foundation of Italian cooking.

He sighed. "Yes, she knows. She told me to stop being a child."

"If you don't want me to go . . ."

Toby took Gideon's hand. "I want you to go. I just don't think you're prepared. You know those old Italian movies where the old people sit around drinking vino and playing cards, and how everyone yells over the top of each other, and there's arguments over the price of tomatoes and olive oil . . . You think that's a stereotype? Just you wait."

Gideon smiled and gave him a soft kiss on the cheek. "Honestly, that sounds great. I mean, my family was never like that. We never had that kind of history or tradition, but I miss my family. So if I can spend an afternoon with yours, that sounds kinda nice."

Toby's face softened. "Oh, Gideon. I'm sorry. I didn't think of that." He gave Gideon a hug, one that included Benson too. "I have some cousins you can have. And Josh. You can have him. My mu—actually, I'm starting to think my mum will take you and Benson and leave me out."

Gideon chuckled. "No, she wouldn't. But I have to ask you something."

He didn't even baulk. "Sure."

He wanted to ask what he should introduce himself as, but he chickened out. "What do I bring?"

Toby tried to keep an eye out on the front of the house, but his mother kept giving him chores. *Take this plate around. Go ask your father to bring in the other chairs. Put this tablecloth out.*

He hadn't stopped since he got there last night.

He'd peeled enough potatoes to feed an army, he'd chopped onions and Brussel sprouts, he'd taken all the good crystal glasses out of the good cabinet and washed them all. And the good silverware, which only ever got used for such occasions. And all morning, he'd helped his dad clean up the back area, not that it needed cleaning, but hosing it all down again was important, apparently.

He'd cut up cheese, three types of salami and four kinds of cured meats, olives and sundried tomatoes. At least he wasn't getting yelled out in the backyard by his dad for not filling up the gas bottle like Josh was. Because apparently Josh was supposed to do it during the week . . .

All the noise, all the fuss. Toby loved being home.

Then people started to arrive and Toby had to greet them. He'd already caught up with most of them after he'd returned from overseas, but there were more cousins, more great aunts and uncles. Even the old neighbours who'd moved away after twenty years showed up, wearing the same old socks and sandals and thick gold chains.

They weren't stereotypes if they were real, right?

His parents' house wasn't exactly huge, thank god for the undercover patio area out the back, because before too long, every inch of the house soon had someone in it.

"Toby," his mum called out. "I think someone's out the front."

Toby put a tray of cabanossi, cheese and marinated pickles on the table, dodged his way through chairs and knees and people, and squeezed his way out the front door.

Sure enough, there was Gideon. He was getting Benson out of the car, and Toby couldn't even describe how happy it made him to see them. "Hey," he said, going out to meet them. "You found the place okay?"

"Yeah, it was fine. Sorry I'm a little late. Benson had a big sleep."

"Awww, look at who's a big boy," Toby said, putting his hands out. Benson leaned toward him with a big smile and Toby was quick to take him. "Have you been good for your dadda today?"

Gideon slung the nappy bag over his shoulder. "He's still a hungry boy."

"He's a growing boy, aren't you my little cheeky chicky nuggy." Toby tweaked his cheek and Benson smiled at him. "We better get you out of the sun."

"Hang on, I'll just grab this . . ." Gideon pulled the pram out of the boot and a wine gift bag.

"Wine?"

"Not for me," he replied. "For your parents."

"I told you, you didn't have to bring anything."

"I'm not turning up empty handed."

"You're bringing Benson. You win every time."

He pulled the wine bottle up just far enough. It was an expensive Italian wine. "Do you think they'll like it?"

"Oh my god. You'll be their favourite forever."

Gideon smiled, relieved, and Toby realised he was actually nervous. "Are you okay?"

"Sure." He made a face. "A bit nervous. I'm out of practice with family stuff."

"You'll be fine." He headed toward the front door when he noticed Gideon was slow to follow. He waited for him. "Hey," he said gently. "If it's too much, you don't have to come in. I can tell Mum. She'll understand."

"No, it's fine. Just . . . what are we introducing me as? What do I say? Do they know I'm a gay, single dad? Is that—"

Toby put his hand on Gideon's arm. "You're okay here. I promise. No one has a problem with being gay here. We can just tell—"

The front door opened and Toby's mother appeared. "Oh my god, bring that little jelly bean to me right now. Oh, look at his little outfit," she said, taking Benson from Toby and ushering Gideon inside. A hundred pair of eyes landed on them. "Everyone," she announced loudly. "This is Gideon, a friend of Toby's. And this little one is Benson. Isn't he just the most adorable thing you've ever seen?"

And that was that.

Gideon was ushered into the throes of loud welcomes, a hundred questions about his work, his moustache, of course, and when he offered the expensive wine to Toby's dad, he was hugged and given a seat at the table. And Benson was oohed and aahed over by every single person.

Everyone wanted a turn holding him.

Carla dragged Toby into the kitchen. "I heard what he said. You tell him not to worry, he's welcome here. That poor boy," she said, handing him a platter of sliced fruit. "Go take this around."

Toby's whole chest bloomed with warmth. "Thanks, Mum."

Yep. He really loved being home.

———

TOBY HELPED OUT WITH THE FOOD AND GUESTS, ONLY managing to catch Gideon to himself a few times. He saw his aunt Carol giving Benson some mango to taste, and of course, Benson was so excited for more, he almost threw himself off her lap. The next time he saw him, Benson was laughing at Toby's great uncle Max—pretty sure it was the bushy eyebrows he found hilarious. The time after that, he saw Benson being rocked to sleep in his pram by Toby's cousin Joseph.

He caught Gideon laughing a few times at something Nonno had said, and then after lunch he found him playing cards. Gideon was the youngest at the table by forty years, at least, but he held his own. In cards and in dishing out shit.

He had a surprisingly good poker face.

"He's having a good day," Carla said. She was washing up in the kitchen, Toby was drying.

"I think so too," Toby admitted. "I think he needed this, Mum. He misses his family."

She frowned. "Do they not speak at all?"

Toby shook his head. "His parents died, Mum. He was raised by his grandmother who wasn't very nice to him. Even his sister—" Then he lowered his voice. "—who is

Benson's biological mother. They don't talk. Gideon wanted to come today because he misses having a family."

Carla's teary eyes met his, fierce and sad. "So sad."

Toby gave her a hug. "That's why I'm so lucky to have gotten you as my mum."

She gave him a gentle shove and took the tea towel from him. "Stop or you'll make me cry. Get the tea and coffee ready. Go on, shoo."

Gideon came into the kitchen, his hands in his back pockets. "They're too good for me. Lucky we were only playing for bottle caps."

"They cheat," Carla said. "A den of foxes, and not an ounce of scruples between them."

Gideon smiled and, by god, Toby wanted to put his arms around him. He wanted to touch him or give him a soft kiss. But he couldn't; not in front of his mother. It would raise too many questions he simply didn't have answers to.

Like 'what about your job?' and 'what happens next?' and 'what does it mean for Benson?'

Toby knew those were questions he'd have to ask himself later, at some point, because if this day had proven anything—seeing Gideon fit in with his family—Toby was certain there was no going back.

When it was time for Gideon to leave, Toby walked him out. Gideon buckled Benson into his seat while Toby folded the pram. They met at the driver's door. "Thank you for coming today," Toby said.

"Thank you for asking me. I had the best day. I know that probably sounds weird to you, but—"

Toby took his hand, hoping his family couldn't see, even though he knew without doubt they were watching. "I get it."

"I wish I could stay longer," Gideon mumbled.

"You're more than welcome to."

Gideon made a face. "I better get Benson home. He's had a big day and he likes his bedtime routine. So far today, I've heard him being called a jelly bean, a marshmallow, sugar plum, and a chicken drumstick, which was a weird one."

"No weirder than a chicky nuggy."

Gideon chuckled. "True. I'm starting to think your family have a thing for food names."

"Only food we like. No calling him acciughe al verde here."

Gideon stared at him, smiling, his eyes full of unsaid things.

"I want to kiss you right now," Toby said. "But I won't because I know for a fact my mother is watching through the venetian blinds." He took a step back. "See you tomorrow night. I'll be bringing leftovers, no doubt. We could feed the entire suburb."

"Can't wait," Gideon murmured. "I think I remember what was going to happen on Sunday night." He wasn't talking about the food; they both knew it.

Oh, that's right, Toby remembered. He was going to do to Gideon's arse what Gideon had done to his the other night . . .

"Oh hell yes."

Gideon laughed and got into the car. Toby watched him drive away, and then went back inside where his mother was, watching like he knew she would be. "He's such a sweet boy."

Josh gave Toby a shove. "You got it so bad for him, brother. You love the sexy Tom Selleck moustache, I can tell. I mean, just look at your stupid face."

Toby shoved him back. "Shut up," he hissed.

His mum frowned at them both. "Josh, behave. Leave your brother alone."

Josh rolled his eyes and Toby stuck his tongue out at him victoriously, just like they did when they were little.

His mother didn't mention Gideon again for the rest of the weekend, though she did give him a few hand-pats every chance she got. The kind of reassuring hand-pats that told him she knew he had a big decision to make.

Which, of course, Toby pretended he didn't have to make.

At six o'clock on Sunday, Toby arrived at Gideon's with a bag of containers full of leftovers. He put it on the table and met Gideon in the hallway.

"Oh, I didn't hear you come in—"

Toby took Gideon's face in both hands and kissed him, hard. Gideon was momentarily stunned but soon relented, smiling into the kiss. "What was that for?"

"It was what I wanted to do yesterday. I've been thinking of doing it all day."

Gideon slid his hand along Toby's jaw and kissed him again, softer this time. "Welcome home."

Welcome home. Two words have never sounded so sweet.

Home.

Benson made a racket, babbling loudly and kicking his legs on the floor mat and rolling over. "Oh yes, you too," Toby said, kneeling down beside him. He picked him up and gave him a big raspberry on the tummy. "I missed you too."

Benson laughed and grabbed at his face, and Toby caught of a whiff of something bad. "Eww, mister poopy pants here needs a nappy change."

"I was just running him a bath," Gideon said. "I was coming back to undress him."

"I'll do it," Toby said, laying Benson back on his blanket. "Let's get this little stinky bean all cleaned up."

Welcome home indeed.

TOBY WAS NERVOUS TAKING GIDEON TO BED. THEY'D agreed that Toby would top tonight, and with that came pressure. He wanted to do Gideon right. He wanted to make Gideon feel so good he never came down.

He wanted to show Gideon how he should have been loved all this time.

So when they fell into bed, Toby took his sweet time going over every inch of Gideon's body. He massaged, he caressed, he kissed. He had Gideon strung so tight, so ready, the poor guy was a mumbling, pleading mess.

Toby had every intention of taking Gideon hard. Fucking him as hard as Gideon had fucked him. He wanted Gideon to feel it for a day or two, to remember. He wanted Gideon to see flashes of their fucking every time he moved.

But when it came time to push inside him, it didn't feel right to be hard and rough.

So he took him slow. Face to face, with Gideon's knees up near his chest and Toby's arms under Gideon, holding him, watching in his eyes when he pushed in deep. The flicker of pain turned to pleasure, the way his eyes rolled back and his mouth opened, neck strained.

And Gideon held him so tight, his arms wrapped around him. They kissed, slow and tender, tongues tangled as Toby took him slow and sure.

They were making love.

Toby closed his eyes so Gideon couldn't see the raw honesty, even though it was in his touch, in the way he took him deep and rolled his hips. But Gideon took Toby's face in his hands, making their eyes meet. "Look at me."

There was no hiding. There was no way Gideon couldn't see it.

And maybe Toby's heart dared to hope, that he saw the emotions in Gideon's eyes staring back at him. And all the things he wanted to say, all the things he'd been feeling were on the tip of his tongue.

Before Toby could say something stupid, he crashed his mouth to Gideon's, kissing him. Clashing teeth and tongues, and Toby thrust his tongue in time with his cock, and he swallowed down Gideon's moans.

Then his moans became soft whining, then pleading, and as soon as Toby slipped his hand in between them to grip Gideon's cock, Gideon threw his head back, back arched as he came.

Toby had never seen anything so beautiful.

Gideon's cock spurted thick strands of come between them, his arse clenched around Toby's cock, milking the orgasm from him. He thrust in hard, once, twice, and tripped over the edge.

They collapsed in each other's arms, sated, sweaty. Smiling.

And for all the effort Toby had put into hiding his true feelings, he'd well and truly crossed the line tonight. There was no hiding it now. There was no way Gideon couldn't not know.

As if reading his mind, Gideon put his hand to Toby's cheek and kissed him, soft and sleepy. He didn't say a word. He didn't need to.

Gideon already knew.

Chapter Fifteen

GIDEON WAS ON CLOUD NINE.

He went to work on Monday like he was walking on a dream, and on Tuesday, and on Wednesday. It wasn't just the amazing orgasms—and yes, they were amazing—but it was more than that.

He and Toby shared a connection.

They were great together. They made a great couple . . .

Except they weren't one.

"You need to ask him," Lauren said, sipping her coffee. They were having a late catch-up coffee break at three o'clock, and Gideon had just finished telling her that Benson had said something that sounded a lot like *dadadadadadadad* during their FaceTime video chat at lunchtime. He and Toby had both squealed.

"What?" Gideon feigned ignorance.

She sighed and put her cup down. "You need to ask Toby," she said. "Ask him what he wants, where he sees your relationship going. It's pretty clear he feels the same way, but the wheels will fall off if one of you doesn't get in the driver's seat and give you both some direction."

"Did you just use a driving metaphor?"

"I did."

"I don't know if I'm impressed or horrified."

"Gideon."

Now it was his turn to sigh. "Okay. I'll . . . say something." Then he made a face. "God. I don't know how. I don't know what to say. What if he says no or if he laughs at me?"

She raised one eyebrow. "Do you really think he would?"

"No." Of course he wouldn't . . . "But if we acknowledge things have changed, then things have to change. Something has to change. What if, for us to be together, he has to stop being Benson's nanny? What then? God, Lauren, I don't want anything to change. It's perfect the way it is now."

"Is it, though?"

"Well, yeah . . ."

"Except you haven't really talked about it, and you're still technically his boss."

Gideon groaned.

"Honesty will always win. Makes for smooth sailing. And, if you *do* hit an iceberg, you'll be prepared."

"Now we're the Titanic? I thought we were driving?"

She shrugged and sipped her coffee. "You get my point."

Yeah, he did. He didn't like it any more than before, but he understood.

"I've got a half day tomorrow," Gideon said. "Benson has a clinic appointment in the afternoon. Just for his usual weigh-in and whatever. I guess we could go to the park afterwards, or something, to talk." He sighed. "Just feels like I'm tempting fate, ya know? I'm finally happy."

"Tell him that. Tell him exactly how you feel."

"Not sure he's ready for that," Gideon mumbled. "I don't want to scare him."

"You won't scare him. You might be surprised."

He sighed. "Finished your travel plans yet? I'm totally not jealous at all, just so you know. Considering my only travel plans include trips to the supermarket for nappies and long strolls around the back garden, showing Benson the leaves on the tree."

Lauren laughed. "You'll have lots of trips when he's older. Trips to the beach, trips to the ER when he comes off his bike or falls out of the tree."

Gideon snorted. "Gee, thanks."

She tapped her coffee cup to his. "You're welcome."

Later that night, when Benson was asleep in his bed, Gideon and Toby were on the couch. There were no cups of tea. Instead, Gideon was laying down and Toby was half laying on top of him, being the little spoon. Gideon had his arm slung over Toby and the TV was on, but Gideon's mind was caught on what Lauren had said.

"Gid?" Toby leaned up so he could see Gideon's face.

"Huh? Sorry. I was a million miles away."

"I just asked if you wanted me to make you a tea."

Gideon tightened his hold. "Nope. Happy right here."

Toby smiled and put his head back on Gideon's chest. "Same."

They were quiet again, and Gideon ran his fingers through Toby's hair. Maybe he should bring it up now? Maybe he should say something now and not leave it until tomorrow.

Say something, Gideon. Man up and tell him how you feel.

But before Gideon could muster the courage, Toby

spoke. Keeping his head on Gideon's chest, still facing the TV, he said, "Would you mind if we just cuddle tonight?"

Gideon tightened his arms around him. "I wouldn't mind at all."

Tell him, Gideon.

"Toby, I—"

"In bed," he said at the same time, getting up. "I'm tired and I'm falling asleep." He held out his hand. "Come on. Let's go to bed."

Oh.

"Sure."

By the time Gideon had changed into his PJs and brushed his teeth, Toby was already in bed. He was in the middle, curled up. He lifted the covers. "Cuddle required. Hurry up."

Gideon snorted, but did as he was told. He slid into his spot and Toby soon snuggled in. Gideon knew he probably should have just said what was on his mind, but instead, he kissed the side of Toby's head and pulled him a little closer.

BENSON'S CLINIC APPOINTMENT WENT WELL. HE WAS meeting every developmental milestone and growing big and strong. Thriving, according to the growth chart. "He's one very lucky boy," the clinic nurse said, "having two dads who dote on him so much."

"Oh." Gideon baulked. "Uh."

"He sure is lucky," Toby said quickly. "But I'm not his dad. I'm just the nanny. Gideon's the dad."

The nurse looked horrified. "Oh, I'm sorry. I just assumed, which was wrong of me, sorry."

"Don't apologise," Toby said. "Honest mistake." He and

Toby *were* sitting rather close together. His gaze darted to Gideon's with a smile that was more grimace than humour. Gideon saw the flicker of something in there as well, but it was too brief to name.

So Gideon tried to cover up the awkwardness with a joke. "Well, yeah. Gay dad here," he said, gesturing to himself, then to Toby. "And he's not just a nanny. He's a super nanny. We left his cape in the car."

Toby looked at him like he'd lost his mind, and even the nurse wasn't sure what to make of it.

Way to go, Gideon.

He stood Benson up on his lap and turned the conversation back to a safer subject. "So we can start him on other solid foods, right? He loves his Farex and he's had some pureed fruit and veggies. He's just hungry all the time."

"Oh sure," she said, then proceeded to give a list of things to try.

Gideon was certain Toby knew all this, but he just smiled and nodded politely.

At least Gideon's cheeks no longer felt like they were on fire.

When they were done, they left the clinic and Gideon nodded to the supermarket. "Should we get some food to take to the park?"

"You sure you don't have to go back to work?"

"Nope. I have the whole afternoon off." Then something occurred to him. "Oh, does that mean you should get the afternoon off too? I can take Benson if you want to go do something. I keep forgetting this is your job and you don't technically have to work when I'm home."

Toby's expression was hard to read. "Gideon, it's fine. The park sounds lovely. I think the day care group is meeting this afternoon. We should go."

Toby sounded so detached, so unlike him. Gideon wasn't sure what he'd done.

Something felt off.

Since he got home yesterday. Since the family party. Gideon wondered if something had happened . . .

They really needed to talk.

Toby stopped walking and people had to step around them. "Can we talk?" he asked. "This isn't like us."

But then Benson began to fuss and he threw his caterpillar, then started to scream.

Gideon's world began to close in, too much was happening at one time and there was too much noise and too many people. "Uh, yeah. Sure," he said, taking Benson out of the pram. He tried giving him a pacifier, but Benson was hungry and tired and that was never a good combination.

"Gideon?" a familiar voice said.

No, no, no.

Dread seeped into Gideon's belly, and he turned around to see Drew standing there.

Just fucking great.

If smug was a person, Gideon's ex would be it.

Toby knew who it was before Gideon had even said a word, and of course it was at the worst possible time.

Benson was crying, Gideon was frazzled, and Toby knew his mood hadn't helped the situation. He needed to be honest with Gideon. He needed to be upfront but was too chicken shit, so he had said nothing and acted like an ass instead.

But then Smug McFuckface had to turn up with his

pretentious coat and shoes and over-tweezed eyebrows. He had the audacity to stand there and look at Benson like he was a nuisance?

Yeah, Toby didn't think so.

"I'll take him," Toby said, taking Benson and the pram. "I'll go find a seat and give him something to eat."

And for good measure, he looked the arsehole up and down like he smelled bad before he turned and walked in the direction of the food court.

Because fuck him and fuck this whole mess.

Toby found a table and got Benson's bottle ready, holding him close while he drank it.

His gorgeous blue eyes and chubby cheeks, smiling now as he drank.

God, it made Toby so mad that Gideon's ex would look at Benson with so much contempt. No, not even that. It was resentment.

The one thing that ruined his relationship with Gideon.

Well, fuck that too.

And it wasn't so much the look on his face as it was the look on Gideon's.

Toby had to wonder if Pretentious McFakeTan wanted to come back, what Gideon would say? He said he was over him. He'd said he hated him, that he'd never forgive him.

But now Toby had seen Gideon's face . . . he wasn't sure.

And it hurt like hell.

His heart ached, and he felt so foolish. How could he have fallen in love with his boss? How could he let himself get so carried away with a man who had just had his heart broken by a long-time boyfriend, someone who had a history with him?

Yeah, Toby felt foolish and stupid, but he refused to cry.

Benson was his number one priority. Always should have been. He didn't want to have to leave this job. He adored Benson, and he loved looking after him.

Toby realised then, with a heavy heart, that he might not have a choice.

Maybe Gideon would come to his senses and put an end to their sexual encounters.

Toby was foolish to think he could have both. And those stupid moments where he'd thought 'what's the worst that could happen?' . . .

This, you idiot. This is the worst that could happen.

Benson finished his bottle, happier now but still not full. Toby opened the nappy bag, searching for the container of rice cereal and not finding it. He remembered putting it on the counter . . . Oh freaking hell! Did he forget it? He was halfway through taking a deep breath to calm himself when his phone rang.

It was Gideon.

He answered the call. "Where are you?" Gideon asked.

"In the food court, by the juice stand."

"Okay. I'll come to you."

Toby sat with Benson on his lap, looking in the direction Gideon would come from, and sure enough, a few seconds later, Gideon appeared, hurried and even a little panicked. He scanned the crowd, visibly relaxing when he spotted them.

Toby swore he could hear Gideon's sigh from where he sat.

"Oh, I was worried," he said as he got near. "Are you okay? Is Benson?" He bent down and took Benson's hand. "He's stopped crying."

"I gave him a bottle. It wasn't much though, and he's

going to get cranky for more soon. I forgot his cereal. I must have left it on the counter when I filled the water."

Right on cue, Benson started kicking his legs and doing that babble-yelling he did when he was getting frustrated.

"Here," Toby said, standing up and handing Benson to Gideon. "I'll be right back with something for him."

There was a supermarket on the other side of the food court, so Toby headed straight for it. He didn't give Gideon a chance to argue or ask questions. He didn't want to hear that his conversation with his ex had gone well or that he was nice to him.

Which was more than Toby could say about his own behaviour.

God, why was he acting like a spoiled brat? He knew why yet couldn't seem to help himself.

He was hurting.

He and Gideon really needed to talk.

He went to the baby food section, mad at himself for having to resort to buying premade stuff. And he'd need to buy a spoon too, because he couldn't use a hard plastic one. Benson's gums weren't ready for that. And why did so many baby foods have banana in them?

A soft voice behind him said, "Here he is."

It was Gideon.

"You were upset," Gideon began. He had Benson in one arm, pushing the pram with his other hand. His smile died when he saw the look on Toby's face.

"They all have banana," Toby said, trying not to cry, his eyes burning with tears. "Makes me gag. And who ever decided to mix beef with lentils and pear? I'd like to see the person who suggested that combination be a thing actually try and eat it. And at room temperature. Christ almighty." He wiped at a traitorous tear. "And the custards have too much sugar. He only has two teeth. Do they want to rot them before he gets any more?" Another tear fell. "I'm sorry I left his Farex at home."

Gideon left the pram and pulled Toby into his arms, cradling both of them. My god, he felt so right. Gideon's arm around him, Benson's face in his neck. "Hey," Gideon whispered. "Want to tell me what's really wrong?"

"Your stupid ex and his stupid eyebrows and knock-off shoes," Toby blurted out. That wasn't what he'd meant to say, but his brain threw it out there first so apparently it needed saying. "I don't want to work for anyone else. I want to stay with you and Benson, and I want to be with you at the same time. I thought I could keep it all separate, but clearly that's not going well because I'm a mess. And the way that arsehole looked at Benson . . ." Toby paused to give Benson a teary kiss on the forehead, and he met Gideon's eyes. "He doesn't even deserve to be anywhere near him, and if you say that he's not that bad, I'm going to be really fucking pissed, Gideon. My family love you—"

Gideon smiled and wiped Toby's cheek. "I told Drew you were my boyfriend. I told him you adored Benson and that Benson adores you and that made you ten times better for me than he could ever be."

Boyfriend?

"You did? Why?"

Gideon nodded. "So he knows I don't care about anything he says or does. Because I don't. So he knows I've moved on. Because I have. He hurt me, yes. But he said hurtful things about my son, and I won't ever forgive him for that. The fact you don't even want him *to look* at Benson tells me I made the right choice. I would choose you a hundred times before I chose him again."

Toby gave him a sad smile. "Just a hundred?"

"A million." Gideon smiled, and with his hand to Toby's cheek, he pulled him in for another hug. "I know we have things to talk about. But maybe the baby food aisle in the supermarket isn't the best place for it?"

Toby waved his hand at the shelves. "It's all awful."

Benson put his hands out to Toby, wanting to go to him, and Gideon happily let him go. "See? Benson chooses you too."

Then Benson leaned out of Toby's arms toward the shelves. "No, I think he chooses food."

Gideon laughed. He found a pouch of organic apple and pear and a jar of porridge. "Here, this will do." Then he noticed other jars and pouches. "Oh my god, these are all for six-month old's? Can he have these?"

Toby took a baby spoon off the hanger. "No. He'll have stuff we make him at home."

"Except for undercooked chicken," Gideon said with a smile.

Toby gasped, horrified and near tears again. "I would never do that to him!"

Gideon put his arm around him. "I know you wouldn't. Sorry."

"I'm never cooking chicken again," Toby said as they walked toward the checkout.

GIDEON DROVE AND TOBY ASSUMED HE WAS DRIVING home, but Gideon surprised him by pulling up at the park.

"I thought we could talk here," Gideon said. "It's a nice afternoon." He looked out the windshield at the blue sky. "And I know Benson loves it here and, honestly, I'm trying to summon all the good vibes I can get."

Toby snorted. "What for?"

"So you won't tell me you don't think being our nanny is a good idea anymore."

Toby leaned his head against the headrest, taking in Gideon's face, and he sighed. "I don't want to leave you or Benson."

Gideon relented a smile. "But we still need to talk."

Toby nodded. "Yeah. I think we do."

They got out of the car, Gideon taking Benson out of his seat while Toby sorted out the pram. Benson needed more food, and once he'd had his porridge with apple and pear, he was very happy to sit up in Gideon's lap and chew on his caterpillar.

"Okay, I'll go first," Toby said, needing to get this off his chest. "After the party on Saturday, Mum knew something was up. It didn't help that my brother is a dick and was making fun of me. In the end, I admitted to her that yes, I had certain feelings for you and things were so great between us but there was the whole working thing hanging over us. She said I needed to figure it out, and I was like, *yeah, no shit*, but then she said no, she meant I'd have to choose. I can't have both. I can't work for you and be with you. She made me read the contract we signed with the agency."

Gideon's brow furrowed. "Oh."

"It's pretty clear." Toby's lips pulled down and he tried not to get emotional. "So I've been in my head, trying to sort it all out. I thought I could just tell myself to be professional and keep my heart out of it." He shook his head.

Gideon slid his hand over Toby's and squeezed.

"I want both. I want to be Benson's nanny," Toby said, smiling at happy little Benson. "I can't imagine not seeing him every day. I just adore him, and I've never felt so connected to any of the kids I've nannied before. I don't know why or what it is. I'd be heartbroken if I lost him." Then Toby looked at Gideon. "And you. I don't want to lose you either. I want what we have now. I want to cuddle with you on the couch and sleep in your bed. I want you to suffer through my family with me, and I want my mum to spoil you. I want more than what we have now. I want to be able to tell you that I've fallen in love with you. With both of you. You're a package deal and I love you both." An errant tear rolled down his cheek and he wiped it away. "But I don't know how to make it work. I don't know what the answer is."

Gideon took his hand. "Oh, Toby. I feel the same way. I swore I'd never fall for another guy. I promised myself it'd just be me and Benson forever because I couldn't trust anyone to care for him the way I do. I had to put him first, me second. That's what being a parent is, and Drew couldn't deal with that. But then you arrived. Wonderful you." He brushed a strand of hair from Toby's forehead. "You, who puts Benson before me, before yourself. You were everything I needed. Funny you, caring you. Thoughtful you. Cute you, sexy you. Take-charge and sort-my-life-out you."

Toby smiled at that. "I told you I was bossy."

Gideon chuckled, swiped his thumb across Toby's cheek. "You are everything I need. You make me happy, like no one else ever has. Even Lauren and Jill said I was in trouble after you'd been here for just a few weeks. That's how long I've known." He shook his head. "Toby, I fell for you the second you walked into my living room and called Benson a chicken nugget."

Toby laughed, teary eyed. He put his hand to his heart. "When I heard you sing 'To the Moon and Back' to him, that made-up lullaby you sing to him every night. It just hit me right here."

Gideon took Toby's hand. "I don't have the answers either. I don't know what we can do to make this work, but I don't want to lose you. You saved my life. I mean that. I was drowning before you got here. I could've lost my job or my house if it weren't for you."

"You would have found a way."

Gideon shook his head. "No. Not without you. You came into my life, into our lives, at the perfect moment. I believe that. We do have things we need to sort out, and no, I don't have all the answers, but if you're telling me you want to be with us, then we'll find a way."

Toby nodded. "That's what I want."

Gideon leaned over and brushed his lips over Toby's. "That's what I want too." His eyes studied Toby's. "I love you. I'm in love with you. I love how you just breeze through everything. I love how you laugh. I love it when you look at me. I love everything you do with Benson. I love how you are with him when you think I'm not looking."

Toby had to blink back tears. Happy tears this time. "I love you too. Both of you."

Gideon's palm lifted Toby's chin for a soft kiss. "Then we'll work it out. Together. We'll go through the contract and see what our clauses are. The contract is a good idea. It gives you employment protections and it keeps that side of our agreement on a professional level. But I don't want you to think or to ever feel that you're just the nanny. When you said that at the nurse's clinic, it hit me because you're not just the nanny, you're more than that."

"I'm the super nanny, right?" Toby said with a smile.

"Right."

Toby sighed and threaded their fingers. "I just wish

there was a way I could stay as Benson's nanny but also not *just* be his nanny. I don't even know if that makes sense. I don't want things to change but I think they have to if we want to be together, and I don't know how to do that." He lifted Gideon's palm to his lips. "I hate that it's so complicated when all I want is just to be with you. Mum said I had to choose, but that's not true. We just need to find a way where we all win."

"Heyyy," a woman's voice said, interrupting them. "Not interrupting, am I?"

Toby turned to see Anika coming toward them, pushing her double pram. She was grinning and totally knew she was interrupting.

"Oh," Gideon said, blushing and turning his attention to Benson. "Not interrupting at all."

"Yes you were," Toby said. "But take a seat. I didn't realise it was that time already."

"Yeah, it's almost two. I'm a bit early. Had to get out of the house before my little cherubs drove me insane." She laid out her blanket and sat down with a sigh. She looked pointedly at them. "Soooo, things here have taken an interesting turn, I see?"

Gideon was clearly embarrassed, but Toby was used to Anika by now. "You could say that," Toby said. "We were just discussing the agency contract. You know. The legally binding agreement that prohibits such interesting turns."

Anika scoffed. "So just amend it."

Toby blinked at her. "What?"

"It's a contract between you two, right?"

Gideon nodded. "Yes."

"So get it amended."

"But the agency stipulates—"

"Then leave the agency," she said, so simply.

"The contract protects Toby," Gideon said. "I don't want him to lose that safety net. We need to work out what happens if things change between us or whatever. Or what happens when Benson goes to preschool, or if Toby decides he should work for someone else? It's fine to say that won't happen, but isn't a contract there to protect both of us?"

"Sure," Anika replied. "But it doesn't need to be complicated. Have a new contract drawn up. If the agency doesn't like it, leave and draw up your own contract." Her eyes got wide. "Oooh, then you could start up your own private day care at home and take my two as your first customers when I have to go back to work in six weeks." She dusted her hands off, proud of herself. "See? Easy."

Toby laughed, but then he thought about it and his smile became thoughtful. It wasn't a half-bad idea. He looked at Gideon. Gideon shrugged one shoulder. "It could work?"

"Um," Toby's mind scrambled. "I wouldn't know where to start. And can I just do that at your house? I mean, jeez, that's a lot. Two babies and a toddler." He put his hands to his face, daunted but excited. "Can I do that?"

Gideon smiled serenely, like a weight had been lifted off his shoulders. "Pretty sure you can do anything."

Epilogue

Toby put the last grocery bag on the kitchen counter with a groan. "You know, it would have been easier to have this at a kids' play centre. No food prep and no clean up."

Gideon laughed as he helped him unpack the bags. "But where's the fun in that?"

"Fun?" Toby stared at him like he'd lost his mind.

Benson crawled into the kitchen and stood up by himself by using the hairs on Toby's legs.

"Argh." He picked him up so Benson could see what they were doing. "Did the birthday boy have a nap this morning?"

"Of course he didn't," Gideon said.

Benson had decided he didn't need morning sleeps anymore, around the same time he started to crawl. He simply had too much to see and do now for such things like naps. Though his batteries still needed a recharge after lunch, for which Toby was eternally grateful.

Since he'd taken up day care, to say Toby had his hands full was an understatement.

It had taken a bit longer than the six weeks Anika had hoped for, but once all the accreditation, legal matters, and home checks had been done, Toby officially had his own at-home day care business.

It worked out perfectly. He got to care for Benson all day at home, and it gave them both more financial freedom. Toby was earning more money. Gideon was paying less—because Toby was running his business from Gideon's home after all—and Toby felt he was on a more even footing in their relationship.

Monday through Thursday, Anika dropped her two kids off at eight fifteen and picked them up at four. And on Friday's, Toby had taken on baby Violet, whose parents had needed a one-day emergency care spot, which then turned into a permanent one day a week spot. Toby didn't mind. Violet was a happy, gorgeous baby, and it was great for Benson to socialise and learn to share with others.

Toby and Gideon then had evenings free, and they could snuggle on the couch and talk about their days like they'd always done. Like an actual couple.

It just worked.

It wasn't always easy, but they were ridiculously happy.

Benson tried to throw himself at the strawberries so Toby gave him one, making him say 'ta,' only for Benson to throw the mangled strawberry when he saw the cake.

"How does he know what that is?" Gideon asked.

"I'd like to think it's the bright colours, but I'm pretty sure he can smell the sugar," Toby joked.

"Da-da-da-da-da," Benson said, leaning toward Gideon. Toward the cake.

He certainly wasn't stupid.

"How about we get the birthday boy into his birthday clothes before people get here for the party," Gideon said.

Toby nodded. He'd get more done without the help of a food monster with cute little grabby hands who was hell-bent on shoving everything in his mouth.

Toby had most things organised anyway. He just wanted some fresh fruit to cut up for the kids, and the cake, of course . . .

"Knock-knock," a voice called out. It was Lauren and Jill.

"Come in," Toby said. "I'm in the kitchen."

Then Toby's parents and brother arrived. Carla was carrying a wrapped gift almost bigger than she was. "Where's my birthday boy," she said.

Toby loved that his parents, his mum especially, had taken so warmly to Gideon. She often said that Benson was probably the only grandchild they'd ever have, so the word spoiled didn't even begin to cover it.

"Mum, I told you not to get him anything," Toby said.

"Oh nonsense," she admonished him. "Like I would get him nothing."

"It's one of those plastic trike things," Josh said. "He'll be racing down the hallway before you know it."

"Don't spoil the surprise," Carla said.

"Like Benson knows what I'm saying," Josh said, rolling his eyes.

"Oh my goodness, here he is," Carla said with her hands to her face.

Gideon came out, holding both Benson's hands, helping him walk. He was wearing a new outfit of dunga-rees with an astronaut on his tummy, holding a bunch of colourful planets on strings like balloons. He wore little red shoes and a huge grin that showed off all six of his teeth.

"Come to Nonna," Carla said, scooping him up.

Toby's dad sighed. "Hope no one else wanted to see that kid today."

Gideon laughed and said some quick hellos before Anika and her husband Sean arrived with kids Anya, Riley, and Malek in tow. Riley was turning three soon and would be going to preschool two days a week next year, but Malek was just a few months older than Benson, and they were little besties.

Then Violet and her dad turned up, and the party officially began.

The backyard with table and chairs was perfect, the weather was warm but not hot, and all the party food was demolished, including the cake, which Benson ate handful by messy handful.

It was everything a first birthday should be.

They had photos taken. Toby's mother had insisted on family photos. "I need Benson and his two daddies to show off to the ladies at the club," she said.

Two daddies.

Toby had never really considered himself to be Benson's dad. Benson had a Dadda, which was Gideon. And he had a Toto, which was Toby. And that was perfectly okay.

"Sorry," Toby murmured as they posed for the photo by the shady tree.

"To-to-to-to," Benson said, leaning out of Gideon's arms toward Toby for him to hold him instead. Benson had started calling Toby Toto, which had almost made Toby cry the first time he'd said it. He took Benson and pointed toward the camera.

Gideon put his arm around them both and smiled for the photo. "Sorry for what?"

"For the two-dads comment," he whispered. "I've told Mum not to say that."

"You are one of his dads," Gideon murmured.

"Not technically."

"Benson doesn't know that." Gideon's eyes met Toby's. "He just knows that you're always there for him, that you love him, that he's safe with you. And if that's not what a dad is, then what is?"

Toby blinked back tears.

"You're supposed to be smiling," his mum said, her phone still poised for a photo.

Benson reached his little hand out for Gideon. "Da-da-da," he said, but then he plonked his head into the crook of Toby's neck, snuggling in the way he did when he was tired. "To-to-to."

Toby gave Gideon a teary smile, and Gideon kissed the side of Toby's head. "Sounds like two dads to me," Gideon said, giving them both a squeeze as Carla clicked away.

No, it wasn't official. But one day it would be. Toby wasn't sure when, but he knew it would be. He couldn't imagine his life without either of them.

"I can't believe he's a year old," Gideon said. "One year. The longest year of my life. The hardest. And without doubt, the best." He turned Toby around, kissed Benson's sleepy head, then Toby's lips. "Love you," he said.

"To the moon and back," Toby added.

Gideon met Toby's eyes. "Both of you. To the moon and back."

Epilogue 2

"Are you okay?" Toby asked. Gideon was behind him, holding Benson's hand as they walked up the front path to Anika and Sean's house.

It was Malek's second birthday, and Benson was very excited for his best friend's party. Well, he was excited for cake.

Toby rang the doorbell and Sean answered, letting them in. "Come on in," he said. "Madhouse is out the back."

Toby laughed and they followed the sound of laughter and kids to a back sunroom. Benson, almost two years old, went straight for the trike, and Toby held up the neatly wrapped gift. "Where am I putting this?"

Anika, carrying a tray of watermelon, pointed to a table by the door. "Anywhere on there is fine."

He put the gift down and found Malek and scooped him up, tickling him. "Here's the birthday boy."

Malek laughed but wanted to keep playing so Toby was quick to put him down. "Need a hand with anything?"

Anika shook her head. "No. But come through here, I'll introduce you."

He and Gideon followed her through to the kitchen. Anya was at the kitchen island, helping a man with some party food. She had her hair back in ribbons and wore purple overalls. And even though Toby looked after Malek and Riley four days a week, Anya was in school. She would come with Anika to pick the boys up at four, but their interactions had been limited. She looked up and smiled. "Hey, Toby," she said.

"Hi. Do you remember Gideon?" he asked. She'd probably only seen him a handful of times, given he was rarely home during the day.

She nodded, unsure. "Hello."

Anika gave her a kiss on the top of the head. "Toby and Gideon, this is Henry Beckett, my best friend. I've told you about him before."

Ah, the gay best friend Toby had heard so much about.

"He's *my* best friend," Anya proclaimed.

Henry gave her a squeeze. "You tell her, baby girl."

Yes, apparently Henry and Anya were inseparable. They'd been two peas in a pod from the day Anya was born. Henry took his role of guncle very seriously, apparently.

Henry was maybe late thirties, a little chubby, a lot cute. He had short brown hair with a dusting of grey and a huge smile. Apparently he was a riot. "Nice to meet you both," Henry said. "I've heard all the good things and how much fun the boys have at day care."

"We try," Toby said.

"Well, we are icing the cookies," Henry said. "We wanted unicorns, didn't we?" he asked Anya.

She nodded. "But Malek wanted a truck."

Henry waved his hand. "So we're making trucks."

"With sparkles and glitter," Anya added, and Henry gave her a high five.

Just then, another man burst in through the back door, holding Riley upside down by the ankles. Riley was laughing, and the man holding him was grinning. "Caught him," he said. Then, noticing Toby and Gideon, he put Riley the right way up.

"Hey, Riley," Toby said with a smile. Riley was a wild child, full of beans and more energy than anyone knew what to do with.

And the man holding him . . . well, he sure was something.

Tall, blond, gorgeous, incredibly fit, and with a smile that belonged on a toothpaste ad. "Hi, I'm Reed," he said, tucking Riley under one arm like a feral giggling football and holding his other hand out for Toby to shake, then Gideon. They introduced themselves and Reed set Riley down. Riley took off and Reed sighed. "I'm done. No more running." He put his arms around Henry and stole a cookie, but quickly kissed the side of his head before Henry could scold him.

"Unca Reed!" Riley called out.

Reed groaned, shoved the whole cookie in his mouth, and chased after Riley.

Anika sighed. "It never ends."

Toby knew all too well. He spent many hours with Riley four days a week. "He's a little pocket rocket, that's for sure."

Then Malek and Benson began to fight over the trike, which Gideon went to sort out, and Anika sighed again. "And you do this for a living," she said to Toby. "You choose this."

Toby laughed. "Playing with Play-Doh and eating grapes while we watch *Bluey* isn't a bad way to spend the day."

She rolled her eyes. "And the fights and the tantrums and the noise and having three kids run off in three separate directions and potty training and cleaning vomit out of carpet. I *know* you've had days like that."

He chuckled. "If I didn't love it, I wouldn't do it."

More guests arrived, grandparents, and the noise levels increased, Toby and Gideon found themselves sitting outside in the shady yard, talking with the other parents while the kids played.

Toby had Gideon on one side and Henry on the other. Henry had finished in the kitchen, and truth be told, he'd done most of the food on the table. There were little roasted beetroot and feta pastry tarts, lemon curd tartlets, and bruschetta. There was also fairy bread and mini chocolate cupcakes for the kids; it was a party after all.

"You made all this?" Toby asked.

Henry nodded. "I'm a foodie," he answered. "If you couldn't tell," he added, gesturing to his body with a wink.

"Don't listen to him," Sean added, shoving a pastry in his mouth. "He does the Bay Run with Reed, and he does it easy."

"Well," Henry corrected. "I do, that's true. But it's not pretty. Reed does the Bay Run easy. I do it while trying not to die."

"I'm trying to convince him to do a triathlon with me," Reed added.

"Running, I will do. Against my better judgement. But swimming and bike riding are a hard pass. Believe me, no one—and I mean no one—sees me in Lycra. Unless it's an ABBA-themed costume party. Then I'll be the best Agnetha that ever lived."

"I'll be Björn," Sean said.

Reed put his hand up. "Benny."

"Anika, you're Anni-Frid," Henry declared. "We will *Muriel's Wedding* so hard."

Anika snorted. "When's your fortieth?"

Henry gasped. "What a good idea! Oh my god, Anika, that's brilliant."

Anika rolled her eyes. "Better than making us all fly to America so you could go to Dollywood."

"Only because Barry never made a Gibbsland," Henry said with a sigh.

Reed looked at Toby. "Unfortunately, they're not kidding."

Toby laughed. "Sounds fun."

"You two should come," Henry said, excited.

"Ah . . ." Toby hesitated. "Orrrr, I could look after Björn and Anni-Frid's kids while you guys rock it as *Mamma Mia*."

Henry smiled smugly at Anika. "You have no excuses now."

Anika cut a glare at Toby. "Gee. Thanks."

Toby laughed again, just as Gideon's phone rang. He held the screen for Toby to see.

Monique.

His sister.

Gideon frowned as he stood up. "Excuse me. I should take this." He walked over to the far side of the yard, out of earshot.

Toby had known Gideon for over a year and a half. They'd been together as a couple for over a year, and in all that time, he'd only known them to speak twice.

Monique was Benson's biological mother. She was Gideon's younger sister. They would be part of each other's lives forever, no matter how disconnected they were.

But her calling him out of the blue?

Toby didn't have a good feeling.

And from the look on Gideon's face, the seriousness, the anguish, he was certain it wasn't a good-news call.

Then Toby had a horrible thought . . . *Did she want to see Benson? Did she want to reconnect with him? Would Gideon allow her to do that? Would Toby . . .*

Toby tasted bitterness on the back of his tongue, also realising it wasn't his decision to make.

He wasn't Benson's father.

The longer he watched Gideon talk on the phone, the worse Toby felt. His stomach was now a knot of acid, his heart felt heavy and sore.

And when Benson walked over, Toby picked him up, sat him on his knee, and hugged him tight. Gideon, still with the phone to his ear, watched them, a sad smile on his face.

Anika sat in Gideon's seat. "Everything okay?" she asked.

"I'm thinking this is not a phone call with good news," he mumbled. "We might have to go."

She squeezed his knee. "Okay."

Just then Gideon glanced over at him and gave him a come-here nod. Toby put Benson on his hip and walked over.

"We'll call you tonight," Gideon said into the phone. "Okay?"

He listened to whatever she said, ended the call, and pocketed his phone.

"What is it?" Toby asked. "You're kinda scaring me. She doesn't want Benson back, does she? Because I have opinions on that. And I know I don't have any right to comment and I have no legal skin in this game—"

"Hey," Gideon said, his hand on Toby's chest. "Take a breath for me. It's not like that. She doesn't want Benson back. She can't just claim him back anyway. He's my son. He's *our* son."

Toby shook his head, but Gideon put his hand to Toby's cheek. "Listen," he whispered. Then he let out a rush of breath. "This is a lot, and I'm still trying to get my head around it. I think we have more to discuss than just this, but first things first."

Toby tried to keep his emotions in check, despite his heart thundering in his chest. He gave Benson a kiss on the cheek and held him a little tighter. "Okay."

"Monique's pregnant," Gideon said. "She didn't know. She's too far along to terminate. She doesn't know what to do. She doesn't want to keep it. She's a mess right now; she can't stop crying. She has the contraception implant, but it obviously didn't work."

Oh.

Ohhhh.

"I think I know where this is going," Toby murmured.

Gideon laughed. "Jesus." He ran his hand through his hair. "We should go home and talk about this."

Toby nodded, his mind reeling.

Anika, who must have been watching them, had a party bag ready for Benson to leave with. "Call me if you need to," she said as they were leaving.

It was only a short drive home and Toby still hadn't found his voice by the time they were home. "She wants you to take the baby," Toby said.

Gideon cut the engine. "She asked."

Toby sighed, still unable to form a coherent thought. They got Benson inside and let him play quietly and wind down for a little while. He'd need a nap but for now, that could wait.

Gideon took Toby's hand and pulled him onto the

couch. "I've had exactly ten minutes to think about this," he said. "And it's not something we should just gloss over. We need to discuss this in full. What it means, how it would work." He let out a hell of a sigh. "Jeez. It's a lot to think about."

"Another baby?"

"It's a girl," Gideon said.

Toby's eyes burned with tears. "A girl?"

Gideon nodded. He cupped Toby's face. "Please don't cry."

Toby tried to rein it in. "It's a lot."

"I know it is. But first, you know what? Your first thought was that you're not a dad to Benson. So that's opened a whole other thing."

"Legally, I'm not, Gideon. I—"

"Then we need to change that," Gideon said. "I know this isn't romantic or how I'd imagined doing this . . ." He swallowed hard. "Marry me. Let's get married. And I'm not just saying that on a whim, Toby. I've thought about it a lot. I want to marry you. I want to make it official, and I want your name next to mine as Benson's father. You are his dad. You're his Toto."

Toby stared at him.

"Unless you don't want to," Gideon whispered, making a face. "I just thought . . ."

Toby laughed and cried at the same time. "You just thought you'd ask me that on top of asking if you should adopt another baby?"

"We," Gideon said. "If *we* should adopt another baby." He shook his head. "I wasn't expecting my sister to call and drop this on us. This is as much a shock to me as it is to you. But if Benson's going to have a half-sister out there, then . . ." He shrugged. "I'm sorry. If you don't want to do that, then that's okay. It's something we'd need to decide together. I can't make this decision on my own. Not like I did with Drew."

"I'm not like him! I would never—"

Gideon shook his head quickly. "No, that's not what I meant, sorry. I just don't want you to think I'm doing this without you, because I wouldn't. I couldn't. We do this together or not at all. Toby, I'm serious about marrying you. I want us to be together forever, as husbands. I love you so damn much, and you *are* a father to Benson, in every sense of the word. So let's make it official."

Toby held up his hand. "One thing at a time, okay? My brain can't do this all at the same time."

"Okay."

They both sat there, taking some much-needed breaths. And Gideon gave Toby some time to get his thoughts in order.

They watched Benson sitting on the floor, holding his caterpillar, watching *Bluey* on the TV.

Married.

Another child. A newborn baby, at that.

A little girl . . .

He turned to Gideon, seeing fear and hope flicker in his eyes. "A half-sister, huh?" Toby asked.

Gideon nodded. "Monique's over halfway along."

Toby let out a long breath, and he nodded. He tried to fight back tears. "A little girl?"

Gideon was teary eyed too, but he nodded. "Yeah."

Toby swallowed hard. "And getting married?"

Gideon barked out a teary laugh. "Only if you want."

Toby nodded and had to wipe a tear from his cheek. "I want," he said, his voice squeaking, crying more now.

Gideon grabbed Toby's hands. "You do?"

"Of course I do," Toby said through his snotty tears. "I'd marry you in a heartbeat, Gideon. Jesus. I love you so much. Both of you."

Gideon squished Toby's face in his hands and kissed him, snotty tears and all. "Are you sure?"

Toby laughed, blinking back more tears. "Yes! I don't know why I'm crying."

"I'll tell Monique that we'll need more time," Gideon said. "There's no rush. And we need to work out what's best for all of us, Benson included."

Toby collected himself with a nod. He wiped his cheeks and took a deep breath. That made sense. It was the logical approach. But . . .

"Call her," Toby said. "Tell her yes."

"But—"

"Riley's starting preschool in a few months, so I'll just have Benson and Malek most days, then Violet and Benson on Fridays. It's actually perfect timing, if you think about it."

"Toby, it's a big life change."

"It's Benson's sister; she belongs with us. No one else." Toby's eyes welled with tears again. "We'll make it work, Gideon. It's what family does."

Now it was Gideon's eyes that filled with tears. "Family."

"Family," Toby whispered. He held up four fingers. "A family of four, apparently."

Gideon laughed through his tears. He took Toby's hand and kissed his ring finger. "I love you."

Benson got up, grizzling and beyond tired, and climbed up to sit on both their laps.

"Love you too," Toby said, kissing Benson's head but looking at Gideon.

"To the moon and back." Gideon held up two fingers. "And back again, twice. Two times, for two kids."

Toby laughed, teary eyed at the bewildered look on Gideon's face as reality began to sink in. "Twice."

THE END

About the Author

N.R. Walker is an Australian author, who loves her genre of gay romance. She loves writing and spends far too much time doing it, but wouldn't have it any other way.

She is many things: a mother, a wife, a sister, a writer. She has pretty, pretty boys who live in her head, who don't let her sleep at night unless she gives them life with words.

She likes it when they do dirty, dirty things... but likes it even more when they fall in love.

She used to think having people in her head talking to her was weird, until one day she happened across other writers who told her it was normal.

She's been writing ever since...

Also by N. R. Walker

Reindeer Games

The Dichotomy of Angels

Throwing Hearts

Pieces of You - Missing Pieces #1

Pieces of Me - Missing Pieces #2

Pieces of Us - Missing Pieces #3

Lacuna

Tic-Tac-Mistletoe

Bossy

Code Red

Dearest Milton James

Dearest Malachi Keogh

Christmas Wish List

Code Blue

Davo

The Kite

Learning Curve

Merry Christmas Cupid

TITLES IN AUDIO:

Cronin's Key

Cronin's Key II

Cronin's Key III

Red Dirt Heart

Red Dirt Heart 2

SERIES COLLECTIONS:

Turning Point Series

Thomas Elkin Series

Spencer Cohen Series

Imago Series

Blind Faith Series

FREE READS:

Sixty Five Hours

Learning to Feel

His Grandfather's Watch (And The Story of Billy and Hale)

The Twelfth of Never (Blind Faith 3.5)

Twelve Days of Christmas (Sixty Five Hours Christmas)

Best of Both Worlds

TRANSLATED TITLES:

ITALIAN

Fiducia Cieca (Blind Faith)

Attraverso Questi Occhi (Through These Eyes)

Preso alla Sprovvista (Blindside)

Il giorno del Mai (Blind Faith 3.5)

Cuore di Terra Rossa Serie (Red Dirt Heart Series)

Natale di terra rossa (Red dirt Christmas)

Intervento di Retrofit (Elements of Retrofit)

A Chiare Linee (Clarity of Lines)

Senso D'appartenenza (Sense of Place)

Spencer Cohen Serie (including Yanni's Story)

Punto di non Ritorno (Point of No Return)

Punto di Rottura (Breaking Point)

Punto di Partenza (Starting Point)

Imago (Imago)

Il desiderio di un soldato (A Soldier's Wish)

Scambiato (Switched)

Galassie e Oceani (Galaxies and Oceans)

FRENCH

Confiance Aveugle (Blind Faith)

A travers ces yeux: Confiance Aveugle 2 (Through These Eyes)

Aveugle: Confiance Aveugle 3 (Blindside)

À Jamais (Blind Faith 3.5)

Cronin's Key Series

Au Coeur de Sutton Station (Red Dirt Heart)

Partir ou rester (Red Dirt Heart 2)

Faire Face (Red Dirt Heart 3)

Trouver sa Place (Red Dirt Heart 4)

Le Poids de Sentiments (The Weight of It All)

Un Noël à la sauce Henry (A Very Henry Christmas)

Une vie à Refaire (Switched)

Evolution (Evolved)

Galaxies & Océans

Qui Trouve, Garde (Finders Keepers)

Sens Dessus Dessous (Upside Down)

Spencer Cohen Series

GERMAN

Flammende Erde (Red Dirt Heart)

Lodernde Erde (Red Dirt Heart 2)

Sengende Erde (Red Dirt Heart 3)

Ungezähmte Erde (Red Dirt Heart 4)

Vier Pfoten und ein bisschen Zufall (Finders Keepers)

Ein Kleines bisschen Versuchung (The Weight of It All)

Ein Kleines Bisschen Fur Immer (A Very Henry Christmas)

Weil Leibe uns immer Bliebt (Switched)

Drei Herzen eine Leibe (Three's Company)

Über uns die Sterne, zwischen uns die Liebe (Galaxies and Oceans)

Unnahbares Herz (Blind Faith 1)

Sehendes Herz (Blind Faith 2)

Hoffnungsvolles Herz (Blind Faith 3)

Verträumtes Herz (Blind Faith 3.5)

Thomas Elkin: Verlangen in neuem Design

Traummann töpfern leicht gemacht (Throwing Hearts)

THAI

Sixty Five Hours (Thai translation)

Finders Keepers (Thai translation)

SPANISH

Sesenta y Cinco Horas (Sixty Five Hours)

Los Doce Días de Navidad

Código Rojo (Code Red)

Código Azul (Code Blue)

Queridísimo Milton James

Queridísimo Malachi Keogh

El Peso de Todo (The Weight of it All)

Tres Muérdagos en Raya: Serie Navidad en Hartbridge

Lista De Deseos Navideños: Serie Navidad en Hartbridge

Spencer Cohen Libro Uno

Spencer Cohen Libro Dos

Spencer Cohen Libro Tres

Davo

Feliz Navidad Cupido: Serie Navidad en Hartbridge

CHINESE

Blind Faith

Ingram Content Group UK Ltd.
Milton Keynes UK
UKHW012016200323
418891UK00005B/66

9 781925 886801